MISCHIEF MAKER

LYONNE RILEY

Story Introduction

Kireth is an immortal, a mischief-maker, carved from stone and given life by the goddess. Faela, a poor peasant woman with a dying farm, summons him to help fix it. Though Kireth is bound to complete one hundred tasks for her, he will interpret them how he pleases—even if it means causing trouble.

But there's more going on at Faela's farm than a simple girl trying to maintain it alone and failing. The crops are withering, the fences breaking, the house falling apart, and not even Kireth knows why.

As he starts to fall for the sad girl with the fierce heart, he decides to pursue the truth, even though the answer might tear them apart.

CONTENT WARNINGS

May contain spoilers.

- Graphic depictions of sex

- Gruesome death of a parent (off-screen, told as a story)
- Death of farm animals (graphic scene of corpses)
- Eating of farm animals
- Alcohol use
- Group sex (off-screen)
- Light breeding
- Light anal play

Chapter One

KIRETH

Footsteps.

I jolt awake to the sound of crunching leaves and twigs as someone passes through my forest. It's likely an innocent human is simply searching for wood to chop or game to hunt. Many years have passed since anyone disturbed me, and then it was only a young boy picking berries.

Immortality has been boring these last few centuries. In the old days, gods like me were everywhere. We ruled the world and kept mortals in their place, occasionally deigning to help them because they made such wonderful playthings. We needed humanity to worship us to continue on.

Then, slowly, the mortals began to change—building new tools and discovering new ways of living that didn't include us. Eventually they stopped believing in magic. In the old ways. In *us*.

Without anyone to worship us, we faded into memory,

which for many of the greater immortals gave way to oblivion. The bigger the god, the harder they fall, as they say.

Now I, on the other hand, am a minor immortal. I have one temple, built deep in the forest, that has long been overgrown by twining vines and thick undergrowth. It is where I rest, possibly for all of eternity.

So, like I said, a relatively tedious life. I've grown accustomed to the idleness, to watching the world pass by. Weeks and months are nothing to me, barely a shiver, the years mere blinks. A decade is a soft breath. Perhaps someday I, too, will fade into oblivion, once the last mortals who remember me are gone.

Imagine my surprise when a small hand tears at the vines and greenery that's grown all around my temple, disguising it like part of the forest. One by one, the branches are torn away, revealing crumbling stone underneath.

I'm fully awake now, curious about who has discovered me and is now seeking me out.

My visitor is a young woman, dressed in a simple dress that looks like it's seen much better days. Her brown hair is scattered and dirty, her hazel eyes determined as she frantically tears off the last remaining brush, freeing my temple from the clutches of the forest at long last.

How does she know I'm here when so many others have forgotten me? And what does she plan to do?

I wait with burning curiosity as she studies the runes carved into the stone. Her mouth moves but no sound comes out, as if she is testing out the words.

Surely she can't be here to summon me. It has been hundreds of years since anyone uttered my name and spoke the words to call on me. I was sure that everyone had forgotten how.

And then I hear her voice. It is like a new harp, a simple but beautiful song falling from its fresh, soft strings.

"I beseech you, O Lord," she intones. Some of her dirty brown hair falls over her face, and she pushes it back behind her ear. She wavers, as if unsure this is the right path to follow.

If I were currently corporeal, I would be leaning forward, listening carefully. As it is, I am hovering on the edge of my physical form, waiting for the words that will manifest me.

She can't mean to bring me out, can she? If she does, there will be chains around my hands, circling my feet, binding me to her will. I will be a slave again, existing only to do another's bidding.

Why, then, am I excited for it? Perhaps it's that I miss the fresh air, or that I have not felt the sun's rays on my bare skin in so many centuries.

"I come to you on my knees," the young woman says, and it is true—she kneels before my temple, her hands clenched in the moss that has grown thick around the base. "As you once promised us..."

She pauses, thinking hard. It's been so long, I'm certain no one still knows the words. This is where she'll falter, where she'll fail, and I will remain entombed here.

"As you once promised us, please grant me your aid, and I will be your supplicant."

The words tickle my very essence. Truly, the time has come.

But what does this mortal being want with me?

"O Lord, who goes by the name of..."

Once more she trails off, and I wonder if she's changed her mind. All she needs is one more word, and I'll be set free again.

Set free only to be shackled.

"Kireth."

FAELA

Perhaps it was foolish of me to make the journey all this way when I could be back home doing chores, when I could still be desperately trying to keep up with everything—and failing.

That's all I am now: a failure, unable to care for the one thing my mother left me. The farm my parents founded, that they labored over while I was young. The farm that was left to my mother and me after Father passed away. The farm that no one in the world but me even cares about.

I say the final word—the god's name—and wait.

And wait.

This is a ridiculous errand. I knew it wouldn't work, knew the old gods were a legend. If they ever existed at all, they are long gone now, lost to time.

But my mother still believed in them before she died, so I decided to gamble. Now look what mess I've made, leaving the farm behind to travel all this way to Kireth's temple, and nothing will come of it. I've wasted my time. I hope that the sheep and cows are all right in my absence.

I listen and wait, hoping. The leaves whisper in a light breeze, but there is no other sound here in the deep woods.

That's it, then. This was a mistake. I rise to my feet and turn around, heading back down the path that will return me to where I left my horse, Rye.

"Going so soon?"

It's a young man's voice. I turn around and there he

stands, leaning against the side of his temple casually, one arm draped over a corner. The look on his face is as if he's the one who's been waiting for me all this time.

His skin is gray, like stone. He has not one, but two sets of horns—shorter ones in the front that wind upward, and longer ones in the back that curl over his head, reminding me of a ram. He has pointed ears and just as pointed claws at the tips of his fingers.

Behind him, a long tail with a spade tip flicks back and forth.

I don't answer at first because I don't really believe he's here. Kireth. A minor god in his own right, known to the valley people as a "demon." He is standing right there, watching me, and wearing little more than a loin-cloth around his waist. Every one of his muscles is lithe and defined, as if disguising a great power hidden inside him.

"You had words just a moment ago," he says with a chuckle, leaning back on the temple. "When you summoned me."

Right. I have to remember why I'm here. It's worked, that much is clear. Honestly, though, I'd never really thought past that. Maybe I hadn't actually believed summoning him *would* work, and I came here because I needed an excuse to escape my dying harvest and disintegrating paddocks.

"Sorry," I say. I can't take my eyes off of him. His tail makes curlicues in the air as it dances, as if trying to entrance me, and he's dragging his claws up and down the stone impatiently.

This is why I'm here, of course. To summon Kireth and put him to work. But now that he's standing in front of me, I'm tongue-tied.

"I did call you." I clear my throat as I squeeze the words out. "I need your help."

He sighs. "Yes, of course you do. That's the only reason anyone ever calls me." Then he taps his chin thoughtfully. "Though you're the first mortal I've seen here in hundreds of years."

I'm not surprised. Mother and I, like her parents before her, live in the far-off mountains. It took me most of the day to get here, to Kireth's woods, and I'll probably get home just as the sun comes up. We've kept to our ways there, separate from the valley people, who believe in different gods and more modern things.

That's why Mother is dead, after all. There was no one in the village who could help her, and she couldn't make the journey to the valley while the darkness consumed her body.

"I'm sorry to have disturbed your rest," I tell him. What else do you say to an immortal being? I am nothing compared to him.

Kireth's eyebrows rise high on his forehead. Then he grins a wide, mischievous grin, and hops down from the temple like it's meant nothing to him this whole time.

"Are you?" he asks, tucking his hands behind his back. "You're sorry to have awoken an ancient, immortal being so that he may *help* you?"

A stone falls into my belly. That is what I've done, isn't it? I've called upon a god because of my own impotence, my own faults. What right do I have to make him work for me, to fix what I've broken?

But then I steady myself. No. I came here and made this journey because I need Kireth. I can't survive much longer without him, and neither will my sheep or my horse or my dog.

"Yes," I say, ducking my head in a way that I hope comes across as polite. "I truly am sorry, but I can't do this alone."

There's no reply. When I venture to open one eye and look up at him, the trickster god is bent forward, studying me carefully. His big smile is gone and now his face gives away nothing.

"Who are you?" he asks, tilting his head. His tail flicks again, more insistently this time.

"Me?" I fumble with my words, his penetrating gaze making me clumsy and nervous. "I'm Faela."

Kireth's grin returns abruptly. He's as mercurial as my mother always told me.

"Faela." His tongue savors my name, and my eyes are drawn to his lips and tongue. Somehow it's sensual, the way he says it. "A poor girl, all alone, seeking the help of a forgotten myth. A demon. An immortal." He walks around me, surveying me, and I stay rooted to the spot. Under his loincloth, his legs are wonderfully shapely, each muscle clearly defined. "And what is it I'll be helping you with, sad girl?"

I swallow. This is where I admit my failure.

"Bring my farm back from the brink of death." I keep my gaze on the forest floor. I can't look him in the eyes as I tell him my ugly truth. "Fix what I've not been able to fix. Plant crops, rejuvenate the soil, help me bring a bountiful harvest so I can survive the winter."

I keep my gaze down while Kireth does another circle, clicking his tongue thoughtfully, that tail whipping back and forth behind him.

"You've let it go to ruin, have you?" His voice is light, carefree, and not at all accusatory.

"Yes." I don't even try to deny it. I'm only here because of my incompetence.

Kireth stops abruptly in front of me, and a clawed finger reaches under my chin. He lifts my head up so I'm looking right into his bright red eyes, and his touch, while strange, is gentle and delicate.

"Why is a sad young woman like you doing all this on her own?" he asks, voice quieter. He's watching me curiously, the way a boy might study an interesting bug he's found on the ground.

"My mother died. She left all of it to me, but I'm a terrible caretaker."

His hand releases me, and I can't help rubbing my chin where his hot skin met mine. There's a pensive look on Kireth's face.

"You'll have to be a little more specific than 'fix it for me,'" he says. "But you're the one who summoned me, so you know that already, don't you?"

Right. I'll assign him tasks to do and hope he does them right, like Mother told me once upon a time. Then, once his tasks have been completed, he will vanish and return to his temple to serve someone else.

I can only pray that I'll have him long enough to repair the farm, and he won't cause too much trouble in the meantime.

"Yes, I know." I wring my hands. "How many tasks?"

"One hundred. That's all you get, and then I'm free of you." He sticks one pointed finger in my face. "And you can't summon me again in your mortal lifetime. Those are the rules."

I get one shot at this, one chance to make things right again. Maybe once I've used all my tasks, I can keep up with maintenance from there. I have to hope.

"Go on, then," Kireth says, shooing me with one hand. "Let us get started."

As I walk back to my horse, he follows close behind.

"I'm sorry I don't have another horse," I say, getting up onto Rye's back. "You can ride with me, though."

Kireth just laughs at that, and it's a somewhat menacing sound.

"No need. I will enjoy stretching my legs again after so much time asleep." He pulls down a tree branch and inhales the scent of the leaves. "At least the woods still smell like woods." Then he looks at me with a smirk. "And humans still smell like humans."

"What do we smell like?" I ask as we begin walking.

"Like stupidity," he says with another bright laugh, bounding on ahead of me down the path, and I wonder if I've made the right decision in bringing him back from his immortal sleep.

Chapter Two

FAELA

It's a long way back to the farm, down dark paths through dense forest, up steep hills and over rushing rivers. My trip here was a silent one, but with Kireth beside me, the way home is noisy and full of his mocking laughter.

"One little peasant girl," he says as we crest the mountainside and start heading down again. "Brave of you to come all this way alone."

"I don't have a choice." Our village is small, and no one would even think of wasting two days traveling with me. They don't much care for my presence anyway, as useless as I am and as decrepit as my land is. Not a soul has stepped in to help me with the farm since Mother died, all of them fearing the dark illness that took her.

"Hmm." Kireth hops over a log that blocks our path. "What if you came upon a bear? Or a wolf? What would you do then?"

"Probably die." I don't even have a weapon on me. Perhaps I should have at least brought a kitchen knife. "But I didn't see any wolves or bears on the way here."

"At least luck is on your side." Kireth grabs a tree branch overhead and uses it to swing to the next tree, surprising Rye. My horse jerks, but I keep him on the path. "But luck may not be your friend for long."

"Are you a harbinger of bad luck?" I ask.

He guffaws at my question. "You've invited me in. That's enough bad luck to last a century."

It seems to me that he wants me to believe he's a menace, that he will do nothing to help my cause. But for the next one hundred tasks, he must do as I ask: feeding the animals, watering the crops, repairing the house. Kireth knows all this, and he's trying to frighten me out of using my tasks. And I understand, because if I were him, I wouldn't want to be a servant, either.

But I've come this far. There's no turning back now.

Finally, just after sunrise, we crest the last peak and the village spreads out before us—a handful of farms and a town square dotted by squat houses. The sun is coming up as we reach the far end of town and keep going, toward the dead stalks and sad, dirty sheep.

My farm.

Kireth's constant chatter dies off as we approach the fences. They are starting to collapse on themselves, too. I've done my best to fix them so the livestock can't escape, but it's hard to keep up. As soon as I've repaired one board, another falls down.

Kireth takes in the dying plants and the dark-colored soil. Finally we approach the house, where the front door hangs loose from its hinges.

"I'm starting to see why you went all that way to call on me," he says, surveying the house as we step inside. The floor creaks under my feet, but not his, as if he weighs nothing. He gazes around curiously, lifting objects and observing the dust underneath them, which has gathered at an alarming rate. "All of this has happened in your time?"

I nod and hunch my shoulders. It wasn't in the best shape when Mother was still alive, but with the two of us there, we kept up with the crops and the cows and managed to fix anything urgent.

"It's an old house," I say defensively.

Kireth tilts his head and his red eyes search my face. "Hmm." He stands up straight then, and spins around in a circle. "So? Aren't you going to give me a task to help you fix this mess?"

He almost sounds eager, like he wants me to give him something to do. As much as I'd enjoy a few hours' rest because I'm exhausted from riding all night, I still have to feed the animals, then see about watering and fixing what I can possibly find time to fix. Maybe this is the perfect moment to use him.

"You're not going to deal with the house right now," I say steadily. "There are chores to do. I need you to…"

Wait. I have to think carefully about this. I only get one hundred tasks, so I'd better ask for something big—something that could take him most of the day. If I only use three tasks or fewer a day, I could keep him around for a month, two if I'm sparing. That should be a good amount of time.

"Perform all of the livestock chores," I say, coming up with something as broad as I can think of.

Kireth's mouth falls open. "What?" It morphs into a

scowl, and his eyes narrow. "'Perform all the chores'? You're going to be one of those people, are you?"

I wilt under his harsh gaze. It's intimidating to be told off by an immortal with glowing red eyes and not one, but two pairs of horns.

"What... what sort of people?" I ask, hating how meek my voice comes out.

"The kind who try to outsmart me." He takes a threatening step in my direction. "Who think they are more clever than an immortal."

I swallow hard as he finally comes to a stop with his face mere breaths away from mine. His tongue flicks out, wetting his lips, and my eyes are drawn straight to them. I hadn't allowed myself to appreciate what he looks like before, but now that he's so close, I take in his angular jawline, his strong chin, the way his nose is straight on the bridge but curved at the tip, with wide nostrils. His cheekbones are triangular and high up, giving his face a playful shape. He's so near to me now that his horns cast a shadow across my face.

When I don't answer right away, Kireth leans even closer, his eyes shifting from critical to curious.

"Do you like what you see?" He breathes his question on my skin.

"Um..." Blood seeps into my cheeks. The truth seems easier than coming up with a lie. Finally I answer, "You are beautiful."

His mouth twists into a taunting grin. "Is that so?"

He's an immortal. Of course he's wonderful to look at. I'm not telling him anything he doesn't already know.

I let out a deep sigh and remember why we're here at all. The windows are cracked and the stairs are bowed, the rafters are collapsing and the walls are peeling.

"Of course I'll try to make the most of what little I have," I say, ashamed but steadfast. "There's so much to do."

Kireth spins around in a circle as he takes in the pathetic state of things. "And you really believe I can help you fix all this?"

"I have no choice but to hope you can." Summoning this creature was my last resort. Without Kireth, I have no avenues left.

"Hmm." He looks thoughtful for a moment as his gaze returns to mine. "Fine. Then I will do as you ask. But I will warn you—the more generous your task, the more generous my interpretation of it."

I should have expected this. He is still a trickster, after all, so I nod in understanding.

"I will try my best," I say, hoping that he won't make my life even harder than it is.

Kireth sighs at my lackluster answer. "It's a shame you have no fight left in you." He swaggers to the front door. "I would like to know what is hiding behind the terrified little house cat you are now."

Then he's gone, whistling to himself with his long tail flicking behind him. I wonder what he could possibly mean. If anything, I am the mouse the house cat killed.

KIRETH

This mortal is interesting, in her own way. Pathetic, really—scared and demure. Beaten down by the weight of the world, almost no resistance left inside her.

But I can detect something else in there, too, lurking

underneath that soft skin. The way her pulse jumped when I got so close to her gave me a clue. There is a hungry animal inside, waiting to be released from its bonds.

A most curious woman indeed.

The one thing I'll say for mortals: they are creative, if not very clever. Little Faela is trying to pit her wits against mine, and though it is brave of her, she will fail. I'll make sure of it. Besides, this decrepit place is beyond my help, no matter how many tasks she's able to dream up for me.

Livestock chores. Whatever that entails. I'll make it up as I go along and take liberties where I see an opening.

That is why I was made, after all. A tool created by the great goddess Lucia, giving mortals what they want but wrapping it in poison for her entertainment. I have a role to play in this world: creating small doses of chaos and sowing a quiet discord in everything I touch.

Milking a cow is a simple task and has not changed over the course of my long existence. I switch from one udder to the next, though these cows are sad and skinny and don't have much to give. When I bring the milk inside, the human is trying to fix the hinges on the door. She's struggling to find the right placement.

But she didn't ask me to help her with the door, so I leave the milk on the table and return to these "livestock chores."

There are also sheep, and if I know one thing about sheep, it's that their wool is very desirable to humans. Perhaps I'll shear them before the summer heat really sets in, and the woman can make enough money to hire a carpenter to repair these detestable fences.

Not that the state of her fences is my concern, or whether she has enough wool to sell for it.

There is a sheepdog who guards the sheep, and when I

lean down and whisper in her ear, the dog gets to work chasing down the stragglers and bringing them into the pen.

I ought to punish the young woman for such a broad request. While I quickly snip off the wool, making sure not to cut any of the sheep's tender flesh, I consider what best way to show her that my rules are not to be bent to her needs.

Ah, yes. I know just what to do.

When I'm finished shearing the sheep in exactly the way I want, I bundle up the stacks of wool with twine and deposit them in the storeroom. The stores are shockingly empty, with only one half-full barrel of grain left for the animals and almost nothing in the way of human food. How does Faela expect to survive for much longer?

This sad woman really does need help.

Fortunately, it's not my job to make sure she has food to eat. I don't need physical sustenance—being immortal and all. I'm only here for ninety-nine more tasks, and once that's through, I'll return to my temple and wait for the world to continue passing me by.

THE SUN IS SETTING by the time I finish bringing the two dozen cows and the sheep inside. I've done what Faela asked for today—and fairly well, I might add. Better than she deserves. I shouldn't have put so much thought into what she wanted me to do. That won't teach her a lesson about using her tasks so broadly.

As the dog chases the last of the livestock into the pen, I throw her some dried meat I found in the storeroom. Unfortunately, the gate is rickety and old, and it really should have been fixed a long time ago. Irritated at my new master's broad directive, I intentionally leave the gate open and return to the house, kicking over a bucket of grain as I go for good measure.

Faela is out in one of the fields, tearing out dead plants and tossing them into a big pile. Everything is withered and yellow, and some stalks have even turned black at the base. There are streaks of red down her face, like she cried for some time and then finally ran out of tears.

What has she done so terribly wrong as to kill off all her crops this way? They look like they've been neglected for months without water or nutrients.

While she works, I lean down and scoop some soil into my hand. It's strangely dark—almost black, as if a deep mold has sunk into it. But how could that be?

There's something odd here, but I can't pinpoint what it is.

When I look up, Faela is standing nearby, wiping the sweat from her forehead. Her hazel eyes connect with mine, and the hint of a smile sits at the edge of her mouth, a contrast to the sadness in her eyes.

"Kireth." No one has said my name in many hundreds of years, and it feels strange to hear it fall from her pink lips. "You're finished?"

I stand up and cross my arms, trying my best to look annoyed. One task should not have taken me the whole day. I will be stuck here for many months at this rate, doing this mortal's bidding. Hopefully my punishments will teach her a lesson.

"I'm finished." I gesture to the pen where the sheep are eating. "See for yourself."

Faela's mouth falls open when she takes in the sight of what I've done. "Oh. You've sheared the sheep."

I have sheared them, all right—leaving their heads and feet fluffy so they look wonderfully comical. It will be a chore for her to fix it.

"I didn't ask you to do that," she says after a long moment.

Anger flashes through me. "You told me to complete the livestock chores," I say cooly. "I did."

"Of course." She just sighs and shakes her head. "I hadn't meant to do the shearing yet to let in more growth, but at least it's done now." She bows in front of me. "Thank you."

I don't need her thanks. This is what I am bound to do by the laws of my existence. Though I expected a bit more of a reaction from her. If I sheared them early, surely it's cut into her future profits.

"Are there any other tasks you require of me today?" I ask, feeling huffy. I lace the words with as much sarcasm as possible. "How else may I serve you?"

"That's all for today." Faela shuffles past me toward the house. "I have to cook something for us to eat."

I don't really need to eat, but I don't correct her.

Inside, I hear a gasp. "So much milk!" When I join her, she's staring down at the many buckets of cow and sheep milk I acquired today. "I can make a lot of cheese with this."

Again she bows, twice this time, and her eyes are gleaming like raw ambers. They are so plain in color, but big and deep with emotion. And her bright, optimistic smile? It makes me oddly giddy.

"It's of no concern to me," I say, waving a hand dismissively. But she remains grinning as she returns to fawning over the milk.

After getting a pot boiling, Faela mixes in the rennet. Dinner is all but forgotten as she busies herself around the kitchen, so I sit at the table and watch. Her hands don't move fast, but they are sure and steady, completing each step with precision.

She makes quick work of it, and soon the cheese is ready to be strained. Afterward, she moves much of it to the cellar. When she returns, she's carrying a few tiny carrots, a bundle of wilted greens, and half of a loaf of bread. As she sets to cooking, I watch her careful movements, wondering again how this one girl managed to destroy all her crops.

Faela doesn't appear incompetent. The fix on the door is perfect, and it barely even squeaks when I test it.

"I cut a piece from an old pail and hammered it into a hinge," she says as I examine her handiwork. "It came out all right."

She also repaired the front steps with a piece of wood she sawed and nailed in herself, and now the steps are sturdy and passable. I'm having a harder and harder time believing that she could have caused all this devastation on her own.

"You said your mother died." I return to the table to continue watching Faela over the frying pan with her meager vegetables. "What did she die from?"

Her small shoulders tense up around her neck. She doesn't turn around, but her hands have stopped stirring the food.

"I don't know." She looks as if she's curling into herself. "One day, Mother just... got sick. We have a healer in town, a woman who knows a little about common illnesses and can make a few remedies. She had no idea what was wrong. One day Mother was fine, and then the next day she couldn't get out of bed. Something was growing up her hands, up her feet. It spread and spread and—"

"What sort of thing?" I interrupt. This does not sound like any ordinary illness to me.

Faela shivers. "It was black, and every part of her it touched, died."

The soil outside, turning dark and useless. The dead grass. The house falling apart at the seams.

There is something wrong with this farm, and whatever it is, it isn't the fault of this young woman in front of me.

Chapter Three

FAELA

It started in her index finger, just at the tip, a sort of mold that crept slowly across her skin, turning it black and wrinkled. When it worked its way up her hand, over her palm—that's when her first finger died.

It only spread from there, up her arms, closer and closer to her heart. Mother was in terrible pain for the last few days of her life. Horrible, excruciating pain, a kind of pain that I think no one alive in this world has ever experienced or ever will after. I'll never forget the unbearable torment of holding her dead hand, withered and lifeless, and wishing there was anything I could do to make it better.

But I was utterly helpless. I watched her die. I wept onto her chest as the creeping black sickness finally killed her and then stopped its steady march.

I burned her body because the other villagers told me that was the only way. They said she was cursed and only fire would destroy it. But if it was a curse, burning my mother's body wasn't the end of its reign over the farm.

Kireth doesn't speak as I serve our meager meal. He eats a few bites, then tastes the stale bread and decides against eating more.

"I have some dried meat, as well," I say, hoping to pay him back in some way for the work he did today.

The demon rolls his eyes. "Your food doesn't interest me. You should eat it."

"Oh. Right." The tail and horns should probably have been my first indication that Kireth doesn't need things mortals need. "I guess I've just always heard of gods eating and drinking." A lot, or so said the stories my mother told me.

"When it's worthwhile to do so." He pushes the plate away. "Do you have any wine? It's been eons since I had wine."

"No, sorry."

I drank it all a long time ago, but I won't tell him that. He doesn't need to know how I tried to cope after Mother died, and I don't want to feel ashamed of it.

Kireth lets out an immense sigh and leans back in his chair. There are raised runes along the skin of his belly and chest, the same designs that I saw carved into his temple in the woods. They look almost like scars.

"What are those?" I ask, pointing at them.

Running his hands down his body and over the strange symbols carved there, Kireth chuckles. "Oh, these old things? Just the words to dismiss me. If you ever get tired of me, you know, you just say them aloud, and I'll vanish."

I would never dream of sending him away, not after all he did around the farm today.

"Don't you want to know how to use them?" he asks, still tracing his body with his hands as if just to draw my attention to it.

I swallow. I know Kireth hasn't always been summoned just to help with chores. Humans have called on him for less savory uses, too. He's known for his sensuality and prowess in bed.

Not that I'd know anything about bedroom activities.

"No." I rise from the table and quickly eat the rest of the food off of his plate. "I have no reason to dismiss you."

His eyes follow me as I clean up dinner, but he says nothing else.

When I go to bed that night, I offer him my bedroom. I'll sleep in my mother's room while he's here.

"Why your room?" Kireth asks, perched against the doorway like he hasn't a care in the world.

"I didn't think you would want to sleep on the bed where my mother died."

With a scoff, he bats a hand at me. "I don't live on superstition like mortals do. I can see what is and isn't. There is no ghost here."

He saunters into Mother's room and settles himself on the bed, still wearing only his loincloth. I wonder if he takes it off to go to bed at night.

"I'll take any soft place to sleep," Kireth says, reclining. "Or a hard one, as long as sleep is involved."

With that, he sprawls across the bed and closes his eyes, as if already gone to dreamland. I stand there a moment longer, taking in his strong, lithe form, the horns that looked so frightening before but now remind me more of a farm animal.

I go to bed thinking that maybe I did the right thing. Perhaps summoning Kireth and bringing him home with me was the best decision I've made yet.

I'M up early the next morning, even though I could have used a whole extra night's sleep after the events of the last two days. Kireth is snoring soundly, one of his arms hanging off the side of the bed. His tail is, for the first time, still.

After months of watching my life rotting like an old corpse, I feel a glimmer of hope. I was preparing the fields yesterday for new sowing, and I'm going to ask my resident god to help me bring in a bountiful harvest. In a few months' time, perhaps things will turn around.

When I go outside to start the milking, though, I find there are just a small handful of sheep in the pen and only one cow. Off in the distance, the dog barks, and panic snakes through me.

I take off at a run.

The gate is hanging wide open. A few of the sheep mill about outside the pen, just eating. I sprint through the swinging gate and into the field.

The sound of buzzing flies draws me to the body. They are swarming a ripe, bloody corpse, with the head and legs of a sheep, and everything in the middle gone.

Bile pools in my mouth. It's one thing to butcher a sheep myself, and another to see one mutilated by a bear or some wolves. My dog has seen me and runs over, barking, to let me know what's happened. There's another body further off, also swarming with flies.

"I know, Petal," I tell her, rubbing her head. "There wasn't anything you could do." I'm just glad that Petal didn't get hurt, too. I wouldn't survive without her.

I send her off to gather up the rest of the sheep and make my way back to the gate.

"Damn it!" I sit down in the grass and pound the ground with a fist, biting back tears. I needed those two sheep. Who knew how many I'll have to butcher over the winter to survive? Will I still have a herd left next year?

Nearby I hear a *poof*! and Kireth appears, certainly by magic. I didn't know he could do that.

"So angry so early," he says with a yawn. "You're making a lot of noise out here."

I get to my feet slowly. "The gate was open, and I found two of the sheep dead." I gesture out at the field. "That's two fewer sheep for the winter."

His tail lashes back and forth, faster than before, but his face remains impassive. I wipe at my cheeks, wishing he wasn't seeing me cry like this. I just have to hope that these seeds today take, and maybe I'll get by long enough to see them grow tall and strong.

"What will you have me do today, *mistress*?" Kireth asks, and there's an edge to his voice.

"Planting," I say. I get back up to my feet, trying to shake off my grief so I can focus on what still needs doing. "Everything is marked out and ready to be sown." I know I should be more specific. "The carrots go first, then the onions, and the wheat in the smaller field."

His eyebrows twitch, but there's no lightness to him like there was yesterday.

"Of course." He makes a tally gesture. "Ninety-eight left."

KIRETH

I do not like how it felt to see her cry, hunched in the grass, her shoulders shivering with the force of her grief. It made me want to crouch beside her and comfort her, to try to stop her tears. It is irrational, but I can't remember a time when I made someone cry.

I hadn't intended to *kill* her sheep. They were supposed to run around a little, enjoy their freedom, and give that greedy human an extra chore to do to pay her back for yesterday's task. My plan had been for her to chase them to round them up, forcing her to fix her broken gate.

This is what I do. It's who I am.

As she dusts herself off and stands up with a grim determination, though, I restrain my urge to assure her that she'll survive without those two sheep. But how could I say such a thing with certainty? I won't be here. It's none of my concern whether she lives or dies once I'm finished with my obligation.

I do what I'm told and sow the seeds just how Faela has laid out. Her instructions are specific, giving me few opportunities to subvert her. Only because my body craves mischief do I switch the carrots with the onions, just to give her a little surprise when the stalks come up.

It's past midday when I finish with my task and find my mistress still working with the livestock. She's crouched by the gate, examining the latch. I say nothing as I stand there idly, watching.

"You're finished?" She gets to her feet and smiles brightly. "You're good."

A part of me preens a little at the praise, but I endeavor not to let it show. Instead, I flick my hand with disinterest. "What else would you have me do today?"

"You can rest, if you like," she says, getting to her feet and dusting off her filthy dress.

"I do not need rest." And standing around while she works doesn't sound very attractive, either. "Give me a task to do."

Her brows draw together in worry. She is reluctant to use more tasks, but we both know there are plenty of things around the farm for me to help with.

Harried by her need to come up with something, she hastily says, "Can you work on the house, then?"

As if she needs my approval in order to give me a command.

"If that's what you wish." I make another tally mark in the air. "Ninety-seven."

She lets out a resigned sigh. "Thank you."

I don't need to be thanked again, but I don't bother correcting her as I head toward the house.

Work on the house. It's such a general instruction that there are plenty of ways for me to interpret it. I know what she wants, of course—the stairs repaired, or the window fixed, or many of the gaps in the walls closed to keep out the heat. But she's left it so wide open for me, I have no choice but to seize on it.

I perform one of the tasks I know she wants done— repairing the balustrade that goes up the stairs—and then set to the other half of my work. I laugh to myself as I do it, at the puny mortal who has summoned me to serve her.

What a weak choice of words. She was more careless than I expected.

When Faela returns around sunset, she stops in her tracks and her face slackens. "What are you doing?"

"What does it look like?" I hammer in another nail next to the hundred others I've put in the wall. "Working on the house. Just as you asked."

Her face tightens as she peers into the bucket of nails, which is now almost empty.

"You used... all of them? Every last nail?" She sighs and

buries her head in her hands. "This is my fault. I wasn't specific enough, was I?"

I just shrug and hammer in the last nail I had held in my hand. She takes the bucket away, murmuring chastisements to herself.

"Stupid," she mutters. "You're so stupid, Faela. Always so stupid."

This earns my attention. I would hardly call her stupid. It was a thoughtless request, sure, but everyone who's summoned me has made a few of those. And usually they blame me, not themselves.

She leaves me there, taking the bucket to the tool shed, and doesn't return for a long time. I sit by the wall, examining my handiwork, but I no longer feel the same mischievous joy I felt while doing it. Her drawn face, her disappointment, has stirred a shimmer of regret inside me.

Perhaps I should pull the nails out again. But immortals do not take back the choices we've made, especially not ones that punish mortals for their foolishness and arrogance.

When at last Faela returns, her expression is hard though her eyes are red. She walks past me without a word, carrying a squash and a few more soft carrots into the house. The door slams closed behind her.

It seems as though I am not welcome inside any longer. Since when has that stopped me? And yet, I don't barge in.

Instead, I examine the animal pen where all the livestock are safely closed in and check the gate. It's firmly closed this time, the latch now repaired. The dog runs up to me, tail wagging, and I kneel to scratch her head.

Night falls, and still the door to the house remains closed. A candle is lit upstairs, and I wonder what Faela is doing in her room. Is she removing that old dress that seems to be the only thing she owns? I imagine what her sun-kissed flesh looks like underneath it, bare and inviting.

Bah, what am I thinking? This woman would never make a request like that. But if she did, I certainly wouldn't mind. I rather like her angular face, with the pointed chin and high cheekbones. She has such a slender neck—too slender, really—and a generous bosom for how thin she is.

It's been centuries since I pleased myself in any form, but clearly those desires still exist. I head into the barn, where the chickens all scatter when I enter, and find a cozy place to sleep on the few bales of hay that remain. Once I'm settled, I pull my loincloth aside and, to my surprise, discover that my cock is stiff and alert.

Hmm. It can't possibly want this small slip of a woman, can it?

I've had hundreds, if not thousands of partners in my immeasurable existence, gods and mortals alike. When my hand drops to my shaft, I summon my memories of them: a beautiful man I found tilling a field. A forest nymph who discovered me gathering in the woods on an errand and rode my cock until she was pink and full of my seed. The widow who needed companionship and respite. Perhaps I even had children out there once upon a time—half-mortals who lingered on this plane for two or three hundred years before the sands of time took them. There's no way to know.

And yet, as I try to picture the forest nymph's sweet cunt around me, a young woman with hazel eyes and dirty brown hair appears in my imagination. Faela's face is blotchy red as gasping moans fall from her full lips. I imagine how tight she would be for me as my hand slides up and down my thirsty cock. It's easy to picture her breasts bouncing as I ram into her, and I think she would have pretty pink nipples with broad areolas. This pleases me.

I keep pumping, imagining her cries and moans and the pinch of her belly as she raises her hips to meet mine, participating enthusiastically. I might even turn her around, press her flat on her stomach and take her from behind so I can bury my face in the nape of her neck.

Physically, I'm satisfied when it's over. As I sprawl across the hay and it pokes roughly at my backside, though, I wish I hadn't made her so angry. It would've been far more pleasant to sleep in a bed knowing she was in the next room.

I sigh and close my eyes. No sweet young maiden like Faela would open her legs for a creature like me. She is probably a virgin, all alone out here at this farm, shunned by the other villagers.

Ah, well. What she doesn't know won't hurt her.

Chapter Four

FAELA

I was so careless, so thoughtless. I shouldn't be punishing Kireth for my mistake. He is a trouble-maker, and I had expected it. I knew the stories, the legends my mother and father passed down to me.

It was my own fault.

The next morning, I'm up early to remove the nails. They come out bent and misshapen, but that's better than nothing. I'll need these nails to fix the fences, and iron isn't cheap.

I cover the remaining holes with old boards so the outside air can't get in and then secure them in place. I need to haul water for us and the animals before I can begin with my other chores.

"Do you need help?" a voice calls out to me as I carry a bucket back from the well. Kireth bounds into view, much like a young deer. He gleams in the morning light, the shape of his strong chest and thick, lean thighs outlined in bright gold.

"No," I say quickly. I will not waste a task on something as small as bringing in a bucket of water. "Tend the crops today. That is all I want from you." Then I correct myself. "No, wait. Please, water them lightly and don't drown the new seeds." They were the last of what I had, and I can't replace them.

For a moment, Kireth looks disappointed, but then he nods his head and draws a tally in the air. "Ninety-six." He skips away, though his back and shoulders are stiff.

I should not have made him find his own place to sleep last night. I was just... angry. Angry, mostly at myself, for being so thoughtless with my task.

What had I thought? That an immortal would be on my side? He is here only because he's bound to be, chained by whatever agreement he signed when he was created.

I wonder briefly how gods are born. Did he come from another one, even greater and older? Who tied him to the whims and desires of mortals?

A little too late, I hope that I have been specific enough today with my request. I can't afford for Kireth to teach me any more lessons.

I take care of the livestock myself, milking the cows and gathering all the eggs, though not nearly as efficiently or productively as Kireth had. I sprinkle feed and fill troughs. Still, knowing I do not have to do the watering myself makes me feel looser, freer, than I think I've felt in months. Perhaps there will still be time at the end of the day to do some more repairs on the house. There's an old tiller I've been meaning to fix, either to sell or to use. It does me no good sitting around, but I've never had time.

By afternoon, Kireth is finished with his task. He lounges around while I finish my work, simply staring at me. It's unsettling, but eventually I forget about him as I muck out the livestock pen.

"You have ninety-six tasks left," he calls out. "That's a lot, isn't it? Hmm?"

Propping myself against the rake, I wipe the sweat from my forehead. "What else can you do? I'm not going to waste tasks on mucking stalls."

He tilts his head. "Are you asking me to come up with my own job?"

As if I would be so foolish now as to give him that sort of liberty.

"No, I'm asking what else you're capable of doing." I have a ridiculous question, but what harm is there in asking? He is a god, after all. I remember how he simply appeared the other morning in a puff of smoke. "Can you do... special things? You know, um, magic?"

His widening smile is like the sun's warm rays after a harsh winter. His teeth are all perfectly white and straight, his tongue bright pink as he licks it over them, and that spade tail is going wild behind him.

"Yes," he says, hopping to his feet. He walks toward me with a kind of animal grace, precise and nimble. "I certainly can do *magic*."

Suddenly he's much closer to me than I expected him to be. When he leans down, a little bird in my chest flutters its wings, faster and faster until his nose stops mere inches from mine. His bright red eyes burrow through my skin to the vulnerable flesh underneath.

"And what would you like me to do with my powers?" he asks in a purr.

My throat closes, preventing any words from coming out. This near to Kireth, I can smell him, and it is a marvelous and remarkable smell that reminds me of woods, of a hunter spearing his prey, of a horse's soft nose. But it also contains a flavor even stranger than those familiar, earthly things. The scent stirs a small, forgotten nest in me, in a place I've only felt awakened a handful of times. Those few times, I ducked a hand under my blankets and tended to my own needs.

"Hmm?" When I still haven't spoken, Kireth leans even farther forward, so his face glides past mine. His mouth pauses at my ear. "Can't take your eyes off me, can you?"

I jerk back. "That's not what I was doing!" I put a good few feet of space between us, turning my head to hide the hot pressure building behind my cheeks. "I'm just trying to think of what to ask for."

"Take your time." He doesn't seem put off in the least.

My hands are trembling when I finally get myself back into sorts. What was that? It felt like all my senses had heightened, instantly aware of his body, of his every move-ment. That quiet, building tickle low in my belly unnerves me.

Right, a task. Something I can use to test the god's powers.

"Can you make the crops grow faster?" I ask at last. I've lost so much valuable time this season, it will be sheer good luck if I can harvest it before the frosts.

Kireth smiles wickedly. But there's something in his eyes that's not so coarse, not so detached as he pretends.

"Yes. I can do this."

"Then please." I bow, as one would to a god. "Please bring me a bountiful harvest, Lord."

When he doesn't move, I raise my head. Kireth's mouth sits slightly ajar.

"You don't need to speak to me like that," he says, and by his change in posture, I would say he's embarrassed.

"You hold the rope. It is by your command that I'm here at all."

And I still feel guilt for it.

"I know that I'm the one who summoned you, but you are still something beyond me." I study him, those supernatural horns and gray skin. "You are greater, higher, and more powerful than I am. It would be foolish and disrespectful to forget that."

Kireth's face twists in a way I can't comprehend. Then he turns around and stalks away, tail lashing irritably behind him.

"I will do as you ask," he calls over his shoulder, voice gruff. "Ninety-five tasks left."

KIRETH

Most of the mortals who summon me are eager to take advantage of me. They know they will have a god under their thumb for the duration of my obligation, and they use their tasks gleefully. It is an incredible power, after all, for a human to have for a short time. Especially if they figure out the secret, like Faela did: that I am capable of more than just the mundane.

I will use my magic for her. Not too much, but just enough to impress her. Just enough, perhaps, to make these struggling crops flourish.

It's been a long time since I called on my small pool of power. It's not much in the way of magic, not when compared to the older gods, but it's all mine. What I want to do will drain me, but I will rejuvenate tonight, especially if Faela allows me to sleep inside the house.

I want to be let back in. This is how I will make sure she keeps the door open for me.

Kneeling at the first row of seeds, I bring my hands down to the soil. When I sowed yesterday, I spent more time with this strange, darkened dirt than I wanted. It is peculiar and seems to host almost no nutrients. It's as if the life has been sucked out of it.

Waking up the seed sleeping deep in the ground takes more magic than I expected. The tendrils of my power reach for purchase, for sustenance, but I find little there. Still, I manage to raise the seed up and up until it sprouts, the leaves unfurling to the sky.

By the time I have finished with the new crops, my well of magic is nearly depleted. I didn't intend to use that much, but these plants were resistant to my help. Something is very wrong here. Unfortunately, I do not have the arcane understanding to determine what.

I understand soil, plants, sunlight, and water. I know how to mix all these ingredients together to ensure success and plenty, as I have worked in many fields in my long life. But somehow, whatever is wrong with this place escapes me.

This soil is dead, spent, useless. I think of Faela describing the way her mother went. First her hand, then her body. *Everything it touched died.*

Has the earth somehow died, too?

Perhaps if one of the ancient gods is still around, one of the great ones like my mother, they would know what is wrong and what to do about it. I suppose that if Faela has not forgotten me, perhaps my mother is still lurking in her temple, too.

Not that it's my responsibility to fix this awful place. I have completed my task, as wrung dry as I am. Green sprouts have emerged all up and down the new rows. I believe Faela will be pleased with the work I've done.

I do not expect exactly how pleased she is.

"Kireth!" When she sees it, she flings her arms around me in pure, thoughtless joy. It reminds me of a child just given a highly coveted toy. "I can't believe it. That you did this!" Then, as if finally realizing what she's done, she peels herself away from me and rubs her cheeks. "Sorry."

I do not mind it in the least, but I don't need to tell her that.

"You doubted my abilities?" I say instead.

She flushes even harder. "No. Well, I guess... I didn't know what to expect. But oh, this!" Her arms spread out in front of her, as if she's embracing the rows of green sprouts. "This is marvelous."

Her glee radiates out of her in warm, delicious waves, and I'm caught up in them. My fantasy from last night springs back fully formed, and I think of what other pleasures I could give her that would earn a gasp like this one.

Instantly, my cock twitches under my loincloth. I try to tell it to hush, that now is certainly not the time, but it is strangely disobedient.

"Good," I huff. "I'm glad it meets your expectations. Is that all for today?"

Her smile falters. "Yes. That's all."

I turn around quickly to walk away, hoping to hide the rather lascivious tent under my loincloth.

"Oh, Kireth?"

I remain fixed, keeping my body angled away from her line of sight. "Yes?"

"I'm sorry about last night. The bed, if you want it, is all yours."

Bah. She is a kind soul, if obtuse. I just grunt and walk

into the house, too aroused to even look over my shoulder in her direction.

With my magic so exhausted, my body is ready to rest. I don't bother to invent an excuse to stumble up the stairs and fall into the bed. With Faela still outside, I stroke my cock just long enough to spurt out across my belly, thinking of her while trying my hardest not to think of her. It's enough of a release that I can fall asleep.

Chapter Five

FAELA

I wonder if I offended Kireth in some way. I was just grateful for what he did—for using his magic to benefit me—but touching him seemed to have set him off, and his demeanor was like a door slamming closed.

Shit. I wish I hadn't forgotten myself that way, just when it seemed like things were going better between us.

Still, after seeing what his magic was able to accomplish in the field, I'm overcome with a lightness, an optimism that I barely recognize. I haven't felt this way in years, not since before Mother died. Things were falling apart then, too, it simply wasn't in free fall. This, though, reminds me of being a child, when Father was still around and would pick me up and swing me in his arms in a wide circle, letting my legs fly through the air.

There is hope after all.

That night, I pause at the open door leading into Mother's old room, where an immortal sleeps like the dead on the bed. He's beautiful, yes. I wasn't lying when I said that before. Ravishing, really, if I separate who he is from what he looks like.

But he is a god, an immortal, a demon. One does not think thoughts like that about gods and immortals and demons. Yet I'm thinking them anyway as I go into my bedroom and light a candle, then lift off my dress and replace it with my slip. There is an ache somewhere deep inside me that thinks intently of Kireth's face, of his lips opening and closing with each sleeping breath, and wishes for one thing.

More.

Knowing that he is unconscious in the next room, my hand slips down my belly, under the skirt. It's not often that I feel a need to touch myself, but tonight, I am burning between my thighs. I remember the softness of Kireth's skin and the hardness of his lithe muscles as I threw my arms around him, and my hunger grows.

I run a finger over my sensitive bead, and my body twitches in response. Oh, am I tense with need. Another few strokes and my legs are shaking, my hips lifting off the bed into my hand. When I slide my palm down, wetness coats my fingertips. I imagine Kireth touching me there and my pleasure builds, the ache growing stronger. Rubbing myself furiously, I bite back a moan, and it takes only a few more moments for me to reach my finish.

I collapse to the bed, spent, feeling utterly filthy at how I'm behaving. A god would never touch me that way. I must banish it from my mind.

THE SEEDLINGS HAVE SPROUTED EVEN TALLER the next morning, and I cannot help but cry out my excitement. Something is growing again, and I'm filled to bursting with hope. I give Kireth a specific chore to do—milk all the animals—and he does it without complaint. That night, I find the pails all stacked up in the barn in the shape of a penis, but that was the most mischief he caused today.

For dinner, I bring out lots of cheese and the rest of the bread, and afterward, I ask Kireth to join me while I work on repairing the tiller.

"Do you know what's wrong?" he asks, plopping on the ground nearby while I fiddle with a joint.

"I'm figuring it out. I've never fixed anything before, but I understand how all the pieces work, so I should be able to do it with some experimentation."

He hums, leaning back on his hands to watch as I mess with each connection point, testing as I go. As the sun goes down, Petal joins us, and she seems to have taken a shine to Kireth, sprawling across his lap. For a moment, everything feels right, the god's wild hair and curled horns bathed in orange light, the sheep and cattle all bundled up tight for the night. The air is fresh and warm, not hot, and I wish this could last.

"It's not that bolt," Kireth says after a while, his voice irritated. Petal rolls over and whines as he gets up and approaches my project. "It's this one." He snatches the wrench from me and applies it to a different attachment, tightening the nut. When he pushes on it, it no longer wobbles but holds steady and firm.

He didn't have to do that. No one asked him to, but he helped me anyway, without even requiring me to use a task.

"Thank you." I resist touching him again because he didn't seem to like that much last time. "Your help means a lot to me."

With a scoff, Kireth returns to his former position, just observing. "I got annoyed watching you trying to fix the wrong thing."

Of course, that was all. But I can't help wondering if there's more to him than a mercurial, immortal spirit.

KIRETH

I was partially telling the truth. It grated on my nerves to watch her try to fix the wrong problem. But a steadily growing, deeper part of me wanted to see her succeed. To accomplish something she's set out to do, and get that big, wide smile on her face that speaks of a time before, when her life was easier and sweeter.

Still, I didn't use a task. That was a mistake. I cannot let her think that my help comes for free, that I will step in and save her when she needs it without her making that sacrifice.

I have been taking it much too easy on her.

The next day, I mention to Faela that blackberries are coming into season. She gives me a careless task: *go pick blackberry bushes.*

I had hoped we might go looking for them together, spending a day traipsing through the woods like fauns on an adventure. Maybe I would sneak a peek up her skirt while I helped her get out of a tangle of brambles. Instead, she is sending me off like a servant to gather them for her, all by myself.

Hmph. And this is how she repays me for helping her last night?

I could carry two baskets with me and pick out pounds

and pounds of fat, delectable blackberries, but instead, I take the cart, pulling it along behind me as if I were an ox. I use my claws to rip out big blackberry bushes whole, tossing them into the cart and then moving on to the next bush. Luckily, my skin is tough and the thorns do nothing to me.

Once I've nearly cleared the area out, I pull the cart back to the farm and wait for Faela to finish her chores.

When she approaches me, sitting atop my pile of bushes, her mouth falls slack.

"What are these?" she asks, brows creasing in worry as she stops in front of the cart.

"You asked me to pick blackberry bushes. I did what you requested." I carelessly lean back on one hand, surveying her from her brown eyes with the long lashes, down to her threadbare shoes.

What will she do this time? I watch curiously as she looks over what I've done again, expecting her to finally lash out, to yell at me for decimating the bushes. To call me a fool or an idiot or a cretin. Now they won't grow back next year.

It would be delightful to see her let loose on me.

Instead, Faela sighs and rubs her face like she can wish away what I've done. She turns around and strides off, without saying a word to me, and I wonder if she'll give me the cold shoulder again and lock me out of the house.

But then she returns moments later, her hands wrapped in ancient leather gloves. Armed, she picks through the branches of the bushes for berries, plucking them off and dropping them into a bowl at her feet.

She says nothing to me as she proceeds, picking one berry after another, until one whole bush has been cleared. Then she leaves again, and I follow along curiously as she grabs a shovel and heads off to the far edge of the property.

There, she digs. She digs and digs, until she's dug a hole about two feet deep. Dropping the shovel, Faela marches to the house once more and wraps her arms around a huge blackberry bush, squeaking with pain as the thorns bite into her skin. I'm tempted to jump in and stop her, but she perseveres, dragging it down the hill toward the hole, where she tries to plant the torn roots of the bush in the ground. She refills the hole with dirt, then stands up and dusts off her hands. There are tiny puckers of blood all over her arms and neck, and even one on her cheek from the thorns.

"You shouldn't have done that," I grouse as she begins digging another hole.

"What would you have me do?" Faela leans against the shovel, propping her other hand on her hip. "Leave them? Burn them? At least I can replant them here, and maybe in the future, they'll grow right on the property. I won't have to travel as far to pick them." She offers me a wan smile. "Maybe you helped me."

I stare at her as she digs the next hole. When she returns to fetch another bush, I grumble as I take it from her, because she is too soft-skinned. She offers me a smile as I carry it down for her and we plant the bush together.

When we're finished picking and replanting, we take the bowls inside with us. After so much exertion, we both dive in, stuffing our faces with the little purple berries. I suck each of my fingers to clean them off, which makes Faela laugh with scandal, and a little blush rises in her cheeks.

Full and happy, I watch her hips swing as she heads up the stairs to get ready for bed, her dress swaying in time. I lick my lips as she vanishes, drunk on the berries and tempted to follow her.

Eventually I make my way to my own bed, where I stroke myself to the memory of her rear end as she bent down to plant a bush.

I have never met anyone who was a match for me, and here she is, in the strangest of places.

Chapter Six

KIRETH

It's easy to fall into a routine here. I work with the crops and Faela takes care of the animals, and in the evenings, we eat cheese and more cheese and occasionally some meat and berries. Then she's able to sell the tiller, and she gives me two tasks to occupy me while she goes into town. When she returns, she has baskets filled with food.

"Things I thought you might like," she says, spreading out fruit and bread and even a small bit of hard candy. I do not need food, but I eat it anyway because it seems to please her.

She has not tried to put her arms around me again, which I find myself regretting more and more. It had felt so good—beyond good—to be held by her, for her hands to wind around my waist and her soft breasts to press against my chest.

It was too *right*.

As the plants start to reach maturity, hastened enormously by my magic, it occurs to me that I've not so much as knocked over a pail in weeks. The idea of spilling some water or leaving a gate open hasn't even crossed my mind, and I don't know what to make of it. It unnerves me.

Faela, too, has gotten too comfortable. Her tasks are less and less specific now, and it's simply that I know what she means and what it is she wants me to do. I understand her now, I think. While her hands move slowly and precisely, her mind is quick and she's not to be underestimated. She has a grand plan for everything, and I'm learning my place in it.

"Kireth? Will you please hand me that knife? I need to cut this cord." I reach for the knife without thinking twice about it and pass it to her by the handle—but I realize that I've been doing many small things like this for her, without even counting them.

"Fifty-six," I say, drawing a tally in the air.

The smile on her face wavers. We've been working on weaving new baskets for the produce that will soon be coming.

"Th-thank you," she says anyway, taking the knife but looking uncertain. She does not ask me for any more small favors that night.

I know she is keeping me here as long as possible, and the more time passes, the less I mind the idea. I do not feel like her servant here. If anything, she treats me like a friend, a companion.

One night, we build a fire in the pit behind the house to cook a lamb that was born this past spring. While we wait, occasionally turning the spit, Faela studies me.

"How old are you?" she asks after a long silence.

An odd question. I cock my head. "Older than time."

"Were you here before humans were?"

"You know the right questions to ask." I turn the spit a

quarter round, then sit back down. "No. I am a plaything, just like you are. Who would call on me to perform tasks, if not for mortals?"

"True," she says. "The world must have been different back then."

I bark a laugh. "Oh, yes. But in many ways, still the same. Blackberries grow in the summer, and pretty women are still pretty women." I make sure to arch an eyebrow at her as I say it.

She giggles and blushes.

The rest of the night, she asks me lots more questions about myself, what I've done in my long life, what I've seen. I steer away from the more lecherous adventures because, for some reason, I don't want her to know about them. I don't want her to think of me on top of another mortal, bringing them to that height of ecstasy.

No, I don't want her to think of me inside anyone but her.

It's undeniable now, and almost painful to keep to myself, how much I want her. But it feels wrong to act on it. She has a sweetness, an innocence, that I fear I would spoil with my touch.

And yet my cock hungers, more and more every day, as my hands and lips and soul do, too.

◈

ONE AFTERNOON, Faela returns from the river, wet and dripping through her clothes. She's been bathing, and as her hair dries, it puffs up into sleek brown waves. I wonder if it is as soft as it looks. While she works on the house, trying to fix a collapsed back step, I find myself sidling up to her. I stop at her backside and run my fingers through her hair, and it's as smooth as a mink's fur.

Faela falls still under my hand, and I realize what I've done. When I pull away, she turns around, her eyes wide, and I wonder if I've offended her by touching her.

Instead, she takes my hand in hers and brings it back up to touch the side of her head.

"I liked that," she says quietly.

I tilt an eyebrow. She enjoyed my touch, did she? Perhaps this woman has more needs than I anticipated.

So I comb my hand through her hair again, my claws peeling apart the knots, and a small sigh escapes her lips. Those full, wonderful lips—how I would love to take them in mine and tease them open. Her eyes close as I draw my hand lower, running my fingers through the strands that hang down over her shoulders. Unconsciously her body leans into me, and I know then that she feels some small portion of what I feel for her: this craving, this need, this itch that's telling me to touch even more of her.

The bark of the dog startles us apart. I regain my footing, remembering again where I am, what I'm doing, and what this young mortal woman is to me.

I want her, yes. But she is my master, and me her servant. As much as I want her, she is still my end point— when I have completed her tasks, I will be free to return to my long sleep. There is nothing truly between us, as there never will be. If I were to take her, to cradle her to my chest and slide myself inside her, I would be taking something precious, doing something irreversible. A girl like Faela does not need such things when I inevitably finish my tasks and leave her at the end.

But once we're inside, cooking some of the greens that have come in, I want my hands on her again. Her slight waist and rounded hips call to me, singing my name, urging me to wrap my arms around her. She must sense my pull because when she turns away from the counter, she rotates into me. A gasp falls from her mouth when she collides with my chest. She reaches out to steady herself, her hand firmly against my skin, but she yanks it away when she realizes she's touched me. Her face is bright red, and I know then that she lusts for me, too.

Perhaps I can serve her in this way, after all, if she truly wants me.

I stop her with one hand on her shoulder.

"Don't run," I say, leaning down closer. "No, sad girl. Stay here and tell me what you want from me."

FAELA

Kireth's clawed hand is like fire when it touches me. He runs it down my hair again, but that's too distant, too far away from what I really want. No, I would feel that hand elsewhere, on other, more sensitive regions of my body.

"Tell me," he says, stepping closer. "Tell me what you want me to do."

He's just asking me, directly, to my face.

Do I say it? My tongue feels sticky inside my mouth. Do I tell him where I want him to touch me? What might that bring along with it? I wet my lips, and his eyes dart down to them.

"Touch me again," I say, feeling brave. I want to know what he feels like, how he would do it.

A low chuckle rumbles in his throat. He takes another step so he's standing only inches away, then brings his clawed hand up to gently brush my arm. It's just a teasing touch, a touch meant to urge me on.

"More." I grow bolder as my heart beats faster, and my belly warms.

This time his hand is firm, dragging his claws up my sleeve as he reaches my shoulder. Then he strokes down again, trailing his fingers over my wrist, palming my knuckles. I extend my fingers to take his hand in mine, but he dodges them, returning to my throat.

"You did not specify what kind of touching," he says, sliding his hand around my neck. He tightens it, and I try not to gasp.

"The good kind," I say, swallowing hard. I know he won't hurt me. "The kind of touch that you want, too."

I know it's not one-sided, not now. The way he so tenderly grazed my hair told me some of his truth. Does he long for me at all the way I've been longing for him?

Obediently, Kireth slides his hand away from my throat, instead tracing the curve of my collarbone.

"That's two tasks, now," he murmurs. "What will you have me do next?"

My heart falls.

I thought he had come to me because he wanted to, because he itches to feel more of me the way I desire him. But I would never call on his obligation just to sate this urge that I can't seem to quell on my own. I am not one of those.

I step away and drop my arms to my sides. This was foolish. There is nothing between us. The image I'd been building of the two of us together, joined in body of our own free wills, dissipates like smoke.

"I will not use you that way," I whisper. Kireth's eyebrows draw down low when I head to the stairs, like he didn't expect me to react this way. "I will never!"

My chest aches as I head for my bedroom and shut the door firmly behind me.

I don't know what I expected. There is no way that a god, an immortal, would ever want someone like me.

⚜

THE NEXT MORNING we are quiet, and I avoid looking Kireth directly in the eyes because I cannot face how silly I was yesterday. When I step outside the house, though, I freeze in my tracks.

The crops have all turned a sickly yellow. It's as if overnight, they have begun to die, from the onions to the carrots to the wheat. I cover my mouth, unable to comprehend what I'm seeing.

Yesterday they were all fine, all green and growing. Today it looks as if these are their last breaths.

I fall to my knees in the dirt, cupping one of the dying leaves in my hand. A hopeless kind of fury takes over me, filling my body with a raging heat. I tear off the leaf and hurl it to the ground as Kireth approaches.

"What has happened?" He kneels in the soil near me to examine one of the plants.

"The same thing as before." I am trying my hardest not to cry, seeing my salvation ripped to ragged pieces in front of me. "Every time I plant, they die, just like this. And there's nothing I can do to save them."

Kireth's tail lies lifeless behind him as he takes in the field full of nothing but slow, agonizing death. What have I done to deserve this? Am I so slow, so stupid, so pathetic as to earn some greater god's wrath?

I get to my feet, and they shake beneath me. Even

Kireth cannot fix whatever blight I have called upon my land.

"I must tend to the livestock," I say, but it comes out little more than a hushed whisper.

"Faela—" Kireth begins. But if I remain here, I will certainly cry, and I cannot expose any more of my vulnerability to him.

I walk away with haste, toward the livestock pen where the sheep are waiting to be let out for the day. Mechanically, I complete each task, and soon Kireth comes to sit on the fence and watch me.

"Will you give me a task today?" he asks, none of the usual playfulness in his voice.

"No." I set down a pail full of milk. "There is nothing left for you to do."

I remember the runes carved into his body, the ones that will dismiss him from my service. I can send him back to where he came from and give up this worthless, impossible farm.

There is nothing here for me. I have no choice now but to abandon this place, the home where I grew up, where my mother and father both died, where everything that could possibly go wrong has.

"You will have me do nothing?" Kireth raises his brows. "Nothing at all?"

"What are the words?" I ask.

He sounds suspicious when he answers, "Which words?"

"The words to send you away. To end this." My heart twists as I say it, but I have no more need for a god. I will sell off the sheep and the cows and the chickens, if anyone will buy them from me. I will pack up what belongings I have and leave this place with Petal and Rye, and head for the valley. It is time to leave the old world behind and perhaps discover what I've been missing all this time.

"Surely you do not want to dismiss me," Kireth says, wary. "I have only completed half of your tasks."

"I have nothing more for you to do. There's no reason to keep you here any longer." I strain to keep the tears at bay, the evidence of my heartbreak. "Tell me the words, Lord. Tell me the words to send you away."

Chapter Seven

KIRETH

She wants to dismiss me. Why does this make my throat close up? My hand tighten into a fist? I still have forty-two tasks to perform for her.

Only twice have I been released early. Once because the human who summoned me died—that's an automatic release. One moment he was tilling a field, the next moment he was dead. The other time, my master had grown tired of my antics and felt I was doing more harm than good. Sometimes I think that old woman was the wisest of everyone who's summoned me.

There are now two mysteries to unravel, but I understand why Faela wants to see my backside. I hurt her last night, that much is clear. I wish I had done it differently, that I had explained how I wanted her to guide what happened next because the idea of lying with someone so tender troubles me. I had hoped she would use her tasks to tell me what she desired, what would please her most, instead of my own selfish passions leading the way.

And now, the mysterious illness has returned and befallen the crops. I can see in Faela's soft hazel eyes that this has finally broken her.

I don't want to tell her the words. Perhaps, for the first time in my existence, I don't want to leave. Not without understanding what has happened here, what is killing her farm. There is a disease, something deeper and uglier than fallow soil or poor management. I have been caring for the crops daily, and I know that I have not made a mistake.

I cannot watch her give up, my sad girl.

"What are the words?" Faela asks again, more insistent. Her voice is stiff, her eyes red with unshed tears. "What do I need to say?"

"Perhaps you should take a few moments," I suggest instead. "You still have many more tasks left." I would hate for her to act rashly and then regret it.

"I don't need them!" There's a painful desperation in her voice, and underneath it, a simmering anger. Perhaps this is the creature I knew was lying inside her, the one hiding underneath her cowed exterior.

There is not much I can do if she truly wants to be rid of me. I can't withhold the words from her. But perhaps I can convince her that there's still more I can do to help.

"Are you giving up?" I ask, keeping my tone friendly, encouraging, without malice. "Are you abandoning this place?"

She turns her head away. "There's nothing else I can do for it. The gods are trying to tell me something, that this land is not for my use. It's pointless to try." She sits down in the dirt, bringing the dead soil into her hand, letting the grains run down between her fingers. "It's time for me to move on. And where I'm going, I don't need you."

I restrain my urge to laugh. "The gods do not care for

this small plot of land. You have not earned their wrath simply by trying to exist."

No, what's happening here is stranger than that. It's as if a curse has been placed upon this land, perhaps the same curse that took her mother's life. Some sort of creeping death, intent on ruining and destroying every living thing here.

"Then what else could it be?" she asks, hurling the rest of the soil in her hand to the ground. "What great sin have I committed to bring this upon myself?"

"Perhaps nothing."

If I have found anything in all my time on this plane, it's that the world doesn't always make sense. Often it is merely chance, which makes it all the more frustrating for mortals who have not come to understand their place in the great chaos.

"Nothing?" Faela raises her eyes to mine, and they are filled with her desperation, her sadness, her dashed hopes and dreams. "Are you suggesting it's all just happenstance?"

I shrug. "Wrong place, wrong time." I don't know what would cause a deeper illness, or what anyone could possibly do to fix it. "That doesn't mean you should give up."

Anger flashes across her face. "I have never given up," she says harshly. "I have tried and tried, but it doesn't matter. At some point, persistence becomes foolishness. It's time for me to end this and start over somewhere else."

I don't like this idea, not when I've worked hard here, harder than I've ever worked for a mortal. I would be loath to walk away now. I'm not ready to give up yet, not when my heart and body still yearn for her. Not when the sickness here eludes my understanding.

I wonder if, perhaps, there is more I can do. Beyond

task after task, might my power serve an even greater purpose to fix what has been broken here?

And would I offer that power to her?

Though my mouth hesitates on the answer, that innermost, knowing part of me has already decided. I will not return to my temple yet, not while I can still make a difference here. Perhaps I can turn the tide and undo some of the pain that's been brought down upon this one girl.

"Give me a chance," I say, rising off the fence. "Let me try to fix this."

Faela groans in frustration. "It can't be fixed. You have already done the best that you can, and it wasn't enough." Her gaze drops to her lap, to her tightly clasped hands and her white, strained knuckles. "I don't know what else you could do. It is hopeless, Kireth."

My name on her lips sends a shiver through me.

I crouch in the dirt in front of her and, with the utmost care and caution, reach for her cheek. I cannot stand to look at her so despondent, so empty of hope, when she has shown so much strength and determination. She startles but doesn't pull away.

"Let me try." Looking her in the eyes, I stroke my thumb over her cheekbone, and she trembles underneath it. What a hunger she has, my little lion, my sad girl. She wants more than all of this, and I would like to give it to her. "Just ask."

"What should I ask for?" Her voice is a tremulous whisper.

"To find the answer for you. Ask, and I will search until I cannot search any longer." I would walk to the end of the earth to seek the truth and then confront it if it meant she might not give up.

Faela's breath hitches. "You would do this?" she asks,

disbelieving but ever so slightly hopeful. "You would do that for me?"

"Never have I met a task I could not complete." I hold up a finger. "Now ask."

I want her to accept my offer, but I will not do it unless she asks. She must want my help still, otherwise I will give her the words and return to my temple until I am completely forgotten, and then I will fade beyond memory and go to oblivion. Perhaps what she truly wants is to abandon this place that holds so much misery, so many terrible memories, and to forge a new life elsewhere. I would not blame her after all that she's seen here.

"Will you ask?" I remain kneeling at her side. "Or will you leave?"

She looks around us at the crumbling fences, the rickety house with the collapsing roof, the rows upon rows of dying plants. What she sees there, I do not know.

"I don't want to go." She dips her head, hiding her face with her hair. "This is my home."

"Then ask me, sad girl." I hold firm. I will not do this unless she spends a task. Those are the rules.

"Kireth." She brings her eyes firmly to mine. "Please find out why my land is dying."

I mark a tally in the air. "Forty-one."

Without any more words between us, I turn and skip away. I must think of how I will solve this mystery, what path will lead me closer to saving this farm. But to discover a cure, I must first learn the cause.

After wandering all around the house, exploring my options, I decide there is only one being who would have the knowledge to understand what has happened here.

I am not pleased at the idea of summoning her, but she will surely know what I'm facing.

"I will be gone for many days," I tell Faela that afternoon, now that I know where I need to go and what I must do.

She shakes her head and gives me a wan smile. "I understand. Thank you." Again, I don't need her thanks, but neither do I chastise her. "Travel safely. Would you like to take some cheese and meat with you?"

"I don't need to eat," I remind her. Not that I mind eating all that lovely fresh cheese, and the figs and cherries she brought back from the market when she sold the tiller, but she should save it for rainier days.

"Right. Of course." Faela packs a bag of food anyway and drapes it over my arm. "Just in case."

I find that I don't want to leave her for the time it will take me to reach the temple and return, but this is the errand she's asked me to go on.

So I set off into the valley, heading toward the sun and away from my temple. Unlike Faela, I am not bound by how fast my horse can travel, so I set off at a quick run and soon, I leave the village far behind me.

That night, I sleep high in a tree, slung between two branches. I hope that my sad girl was able to finish the chores today without me. When I remember the softness of her hair under my hand, my cock snaps to attention, and I'm forced to pump out a full, sticky white load in the middle of the woods before I can fall asleep.

Without a soft bed to rest on, I move slower the next day, so I draw lightly on my well of magic to speed up my pace. I will refill it when I return home.

Home.

That is a strange word, and not one I've ever used to

refer to a place that is not my temple. And yet somehow, in the last few weeks, that rickety house and the hard bed have become my own. I've grown accustomed to waking up to Faela's voice as she calls to Petal out in the field, and without it, I feel strange. Different. Not quite like myself.

I wonder what has happened to me.

At the end of the second day, the smell of the sea tells me I'm close to my destination. My mother's temple lies high on a cliff overlooking the ocean, where her husband, my father, once ruled. I believe he has already gone on to oblivion, forgotten by the sailors who once prayed to him.

I hope that my mother is still there, that the belief of small people like Faela has kept her bound to this plane.

The towering columns of the shrine come into sight, and I run the rest of the way to the top of the cliff. The sun is starting to set, its rays spreading like a fan across the ocean. I walk up the many dozen steps to my great mother's temple and approach the statue of her that stands at the center. It is not a very good likeness, but it will suffice to summon her.

I try to act casual as I approach. If there is one rule with gods, it is that they cannot and should not know your weaknesses. Even my mother has a vengeful side, with a meddling nature that can make her fearsome.

"Great goddess Lucia," I begin, saying the words from memory. "Come to my aid, O mysterious mother of the Earth."

I recite the rest of her long-winded summoning, and when I'm finished, I fall silent and wait. I can't detect her presence here, but she is likely too weak to give off much of an aura. I wait some more and kick a rock, looking off toward the mountains where the farm is waiting for my return.

"You would deface my temple this way?" a deep woman's voice asks me.

I turn around to face her slowly, tucking my hands behind my back. There she is—my mother, the goddess who carved me from a stone so many eons ago. She had wanted another toy for her entertainment, and I was an ideal way to challenge mortals with their own desires. She molded me into the perfect tool to torment them.

Her long gown trails across the stone floor behind her as she approaches me, waves of blonde hair cascading down her back. Voluptuous and beautiful. And dangerous.

"Kireth. I did not expect you." She takes a lock of my hair in her hand and curls it around her finger. "If you are here, then you have been summoned, which means you have ventured out on what, one of your tasks?"

I smirk at her, knowing I must keep my true intentions here veiled.

"Indeed." I roll my eyes a little just for flavor.

She tilts her head. "No happy reunion, then? No asking how your mother has been all this time?"

"You were here, I assumed," I say, and she shoots me a dark look. I ought not to push her too far if I want her help, though.

"Idling while the humans forget," she says. "But they haven't forgotten you, have they?" I detect some jealousy in her voice. "What is your question, then, foolish Kireth?"

I crack my knuckles. I hope she can solve this mystery for me.

"There is a farm two days' travel from here," I begin. "It has been beset upon by a curse of some kind. Crops will not grow. Animals are sickly. Everything dies."

She nods, as if this is all very routine. "It sounds like a curse to me," she says. "So, where is the question?"

I huff. I was getting to it. "How do I stop it?"

Her surprise is apparent. "Stop it? Why would you care about that, my wild son?"

"My task is to find a way to save this farm from obliteration."

She arches an eyebrow. "Such a generous request," she says, and she sounds suspicious. "And your first thought was to come and summon me?"

I sigh impatiently. "The mortal has been very specific," I say, and for the most part, that's been true. "I have waylaid her quest many times before she thought to ask me to come to you." I hope Lucia doesn't detect my lie.

"Ah. You've been outsmarted." This makes her smile. "Your master must be a clever one indeed."

I just shrug disaffectedly. "So, do you know what would cause soil to rot? What would strike a human down with a black mold?"

These words catch her attention. "It killed a human? That is a powerful curse." She closes her eyes and holds up her hands to indicate I should stay silent. A little hum rumbles in her throat, and her hands flutter back to her sides. The air ripples between us.

Suddenly her eyes open. "Oh." They land on me, and a wide, wicked smile crosses her face.

I don't like it. I don't like it at all.

"You angered someone," she says. "Yes, I found your farm. And yes, it is cursed."

"By whom?" I ask, too eagerly. Her smile spreads. I fear that I've been found out for something, but I'm not sure what.

"Someone who had a bone to pick with you, once upon a time." She laughs in a way that's certainly not kind. "You are truly an awful thing."

"You should know," I growl. "You made me."

But who has done it? Who could I have harmed in the past that they would find this place, this woman, and inflict death upon them?

"I see. So you do not remember." Lucia is much taller than I and has to lean down to push the hair back behind my horns. If Faela were here, my mother would be twice her size. "How many have you wronged over the course of your long life that a single grudge would not stand out to you?" Her laugh is not kind. "There was once an oracle, was there not?"

At first the word means nothing to me. I try to think back to a time of oracles, when I might have met one.

And then I remember with a burst of clarity. Oh, that is not a story I want to revisit.

I can see why the oracle would have had a grudge against me. But I completed my one hundred tasks not long after my run-in with her, and so I returned to my entombment in the temple—which I thought had freed me from the repercussions.

"But why did she choose this farm?" I need to know what this all has to do with Faela's home. Why would the oracle have targeted this one unfortunate girl, so far in the future, with a curse? The oracle herself is long gone, and yet her magic remains.

"Because she was an *oracle*, you fool," Lucia says, whacking me across the head. I reel back, clutching my ear, and hiss at her. "She knew when your chosen one would arrive. When her curse would hurt you the most."

My... chosen one?

There's a tinkle of laughter as I ponder this. Who could she mean? There is no *chosen one* for me, no creature picked by fate to be mine.

My mother looks simply radiant at my discomfort. "The one you were fated to meet," she says, leaning down close to whisper in my ear. "The oracle knew the girl you would fall for, and so she struck you closest to your heart."

It hits me like a blunt weapon to the head.

My sad girl. Oh, I do understand now. All the smiles I hoard like a dragon, all the times my chest ached with her losses—the oracle knew that Faela would be the one to capture me, which also makes her the most capable of hurting me, and so that is who she targeted with her wrath.

"What can I do?" I ask, and my facade is forgotten because Lucia already knows the truth, probably deeper than I do. "How do I stop it?"

The goddess pouts. "So demanding." She gestures with one hand, and an invisible wind pushes me backward, sliding me into a chair that has emerged from the stone. "Stopping a curse isn't easy."

She produces a piece of paper and writes. Her hand is unnaturally quick, and she finishes with a swish of her quill before handing me the paper.

"Follow these instructions to create a potion. Pour a droplet on the ground every day for many days, and it will force the curse to retreat. You must have a way to capture it, or it may simply run off and return later. Use a container that closes with a lock, and do not let it out."

Lucia is offering me so much information that I'm surprised. I got my capricious nature from her. Surely she has no reason to help me.

"Why do you assist me with this?" I ask, tucking the paper away. There must be a catch of some kind.

My mother gasps with offense. "I'm not allowed to help my own son? Without him being suspicious of my motives?"

"You always have a motive," I say.

"My motive is to see you happy, Kireth." She leans down and squeezes the skin of my cheek, much harder than necessary. "But remember, you only have forty-one tasks left. And then your time there is up, chosen one or not."

Right. I know.

"Thank you for the lesson," I grunt. "I must be going now if I'm to gather all of this."

Lucia just rubs her chin thoughtfully. "A purely trans-actional visit from a child? Who could have imagined."

"It was good to see you, Mother," I say, and I'm the tiniest bit honest, because despite the pain that comes with the truth, now I know how to help Faela.

"You too, Kireth." She arches a brow at me. "Remember: forty-one."

Chapter Eight

FAELA

It's been nearly five days since Kireth left, and I feel his absence acutely. I had gotten so accustomed to his chatter, his energetic presence, that it feels lonely and rather quiet without him around. With the crops all withering, there is little to do but attend to the livestock.

Has this immortal really become so important to me that I miss his companionship? I cannot get attached to him. When his tasks are spent and his time is up, he will leave me.

At the end of the fifth day, though, I hear Kireth's singsong voice carry across the farm to where I'm spreading hay in the pen.

"Sad girl!" he calls out, springing into view as he comes down the road. "Where are you?"

I run to the fence and climb over it, and when he sees me, Kireth grins widely. I'm tempted to throw my arms around him, but I restrain myself.

"I've done as you asked," he says, holding up the bag I'd given him when he left, "and I return bearing the solution."

My heart leaps. So there is an answer to all of this. In the time that he's been gone, the plants have further wilted and died, and now many of the stalks are black with sickness. I only hope that some of them can be saved with this cure he's found.

"Thank you, thank you!" I could just kiss his face. "I don't know what you did, but thank you."

He wags a finger at me. "Don't thank me until it works. And even then, don't thank me. I'm doing what you asked." He gestures at the house. "When you're finished out here, let's go inside. I have to brew a potion."

I quickly wrap up my chores and gallop in through the front door. I don't realize how much I've missed Kireth until he turns and smiles at me, that big, mischievous, enigmatic grin filling my heart with warm hope, and... longing. The need I'd felt for him the night before he left comes roaring back.

"My sad girl," he says, crossing the distance between us. He lifts a finger to my face and runs it along my cheekbone. "Did you miss me?"

My mouth opens and closes, but no sound escapes. Of course I missed him. I missed his laughter, his jokes, his smiles. But I can't tell him the truth, can I? And reveal just how weak I've become for him?

But a knowing look crosses his face as he watches me.

"Ah, I see." His finger trails down from my cheek to my lips, and I gasp in surprise as he traces the seam of them.

Then I remember the potion. If there's a way to bring back my farm, we must act quickly.

"Wait." I sound a little breathless as I plant both my feet

firmly on the ground. "What did you bring back? What do we need to do?"

Kireth blinks, as if he had forgotten. "Oh, right." It's with some reluctance that his hand leaves my mouth. He draws open the bag on the table, revealing an assortment of odd ingredients—plants, herbs, nuts, the corpse of a frog, a pinecone, a tiny bird's egg, and a strange beetle I've never seen before. "Took me a while to find all of this."

I peer down at everything he's gathered. "What do we do with it?"

Kireth pulls a note out of his loincloth, and I wonder how that works. Does he have a pocket in there?

"I have a recipe." He looks at me expectantly. "Should I make it?"

"Yes!" It comes out more forcefully than I'd intended. "I mean, yes. Please make it."

"Forty," he says, tallying in the air, and turns back to the table to begin.

There's a lot of grinding with the mortar and pestle, and then Kireth asks me to retrieve some cold water from the river. When I return, he's gutted the frog and mixed the innards up with the beetle and egg, along with the other brown-green mess. He adds some of the fresh water to the mixture and it's an awful color as he swirls it around.

"Every day, you must put a few drops of this around the farm," he tells me firmly, handing me the bowl. "Everywhere that's been affected by this plague." He takes out a drop with one finger and brings it to the creaky, splintering wooden floorboards.

"Even inside the house?" I ask.

He grins. "This place isn't falling apart because of your caretaking. It's falling apart because a curse is killing it, as it is killing everything on this land."

"A curse?" What did he discover while he was gone? Where did he go that he found this solution?

When Kireth touches his finger to the floor, the droplet of potion sizzles. He draws his hand away quickly, and the spot emanates a soft glow. As soon as it began, the glow fades, and I wonder if it's just my imagination that the floor now looks cleaner in that spot.

"There." Kireth hands me the bowl. "Go spread some around. We will do this every day until the curse starts to loosen its hold on the farm. Once we have it on the run, we must capture it."

That is all very curious. I didn't know curses were the type of things to get up and run away.

"How did you find this out?" I ask. "What is the nature of this curse?"

The pleasure and mischief fades from his face. "You should go take care of it right away."

I note his dodge of my question, and pledge to myself that I'll bring it up again later. I wonder if Kireth knows what we did to earn this curse, what my parents might have done to bring this wrath down upon us.

I do as I'm told and sprinkle the potion around the field, then the livestock pens. Once I'm finished, I return to the house to find Kireth gone. Instead, laughter rolls up the hill from the nearby river, and I would know that sound anywhere.

When I reach the riverbank, he is in the water, loincloth lying on the ground just at the edge. He lets out a whoop when I appear and splashes water in my direction.

"Come in," he purrs. "I thought I could use a bath after all that travel."

"I don't need one." I can't imagine taking my clothes off in front of a god. It would be uncouth.

Kireth arches an eyebrow. "Oh? Are you modest, dear human? As if I haven't already seen many young maidens' bodies before."

I dislike the sound of that. Other maidens whose naked bodies he's partaken in? My expression must show, because Kireth sighs and swims closer.

"But none of them were as fair as you," he says with a wide grin.

"I bet you say that to everyone."

He has surely pleasured many women in his innumerable years and probably made them all feel quite special.

Instead of answering, Kireth rises from the water. Now he's naked in front of me, and my eyes are drawn against my will to the place between his legs. A long, gray penis hangs there, the rounded head covered by dark skin.

I gasp. Though I've never touched one, I have seen them before when I bathed with the village boys many, many years ago—and those were nothing in comparison to this.

A fiery inferno lights in my belly. I know where an object like that fits, and that place inside me is throbbing.

With one deft arm, Kireth reaches out and catches me. He draws me in closer, until I'm just inches away from his face, our chests almost touching. After inhaling a long breath of me, he lets out a sigh of relief.

"My sad girl," he says quietly, and lifts his hand to run it through my hair. His touch is so soft and inviting that I instinctively lean into it, and I feel his claws tighten around a thick lock. His breathing shallows, and it's not until he leans toward me, holding me up with one arm around my back, that I realize he's going to kiss me.

"Kireth?" I ask, uncertain. What is the price of this touch? As much as I crave him, for his clever mouth and lithe, flawless body, I cannot—and will not—use my tasks to suit my own carnal needs.

He pauses, and I can feel his breath on my lips.

"What is it?" he asks. Those red eyes of his bore into me. "Don't you desire this, too?"

Oh, I do. More than anything, I do.

"I can't pay," I say, drawing back. His arm doesn't release me. "I won't use you that way."

Kireth's curious expression doesn't falter. Instead, it shifts into a kind of regretful smile.

"Then this time, I won't ask you to." He draws me closer. "I will give myself quite freely, if that is what you want." His clawed hand roves over my hip, saying all the same words as his mouth, and I want more of it—more, more. I want to know what Kireth tastes like, what he would do with me if he could do anything he wanted. His hand is just a taste, a sampling of what could come later.

I need the full meal.

"Faela." Kireth's voice startles me, and I realize I've been staring for some time. "You are fairer than any woman I've ever laid eyes on. And this is the truth." His fingers twine with mine, and he brings them up to his lips. In his eyes, I think I see a budding shyness, a quiet fear that I might reject him.

But I want him. If I were to give myself anything I dreamed of, it would be to feel my own naked body pressed flush against his.

"Will you join me?" he asks, tugging my hand gently toward the water. "Let me wash your hair. Please. It will cost nothing."

My words fall back into my chest because it feels too scandalous to let them out. Yes, I want to be naked with him. Most certainly. But wouldn't it be terribly lecherous of me to say it out loud? Instead I nod and reach for the hem of my dress. A wide smile spreads across Kireth's face as I pull it upward, then bring it over my head and arms. Underneath is my slip, and the demon's eyes rove over me hungrily as I rid myself of that, too.

Now I'm bared to him, and it's cold, so my nipples are tight and hard. Kireth leads me down the bank as he backs up into the river, drawing me along until the water is up to my hips, and I'm relieved to at least have my most private parts hidden.

Kireth tugs me even closer to him, and I follow without resistance. I want him nearer, too. I long to feel that ash-gray skin with the twirling markings carved into it pressed against mine.

Then he wraps his other arm around me, and my wish is granted. The gap between our bodies closes, and Kireth brings my head to nestle in the crook of his neck as he embraces me. His nose nuzzles my hair, and his claws comb through it as if I am a precious and beloved thing. Slowly he kneels, bringing me down with him into the river until we are both under the surface of the water, surrounded by each other's bodies.

Then, at last, he kisses me.

KIRETH

If this is all I get of her, that will be enough.

Faela's lips are as soft as butter, as sweet as honey, and they sate a thirst in me I didn't know I had. She's tentative and shy, and I wonder if my sad girl has ever been kissed before.

There is so much I don't yet know about her, but I will learn it.

I draw her further in, weaving her legs around my hips, showing her where to tangle her hands in my hair as I kiss her with every last ounce of my patience and restraint. I will need to take it slow for her, leading her deeper like one would guide a foal across a stream, for as long as she wants to come with me.

After she's settled in my lap, Faela relaxes against me. I draw my tongue across her lips, and she lets out a surprised gasp. With this opening, I sweep inside her mouth, showing her how this silky appendage could be used to pleasure her. I suckle her, paying attention to every corner until her lips are open for me and her tongue is tangling with mine. She shudders under my hands, letting out the tiniest of moans as I teach her mouth how to dance.

While I tease her in one place, I wander across her naked skin, brushing my thumbs past the plump curve of her breasts down to the swell of her behind. I've been trying to keep my cock under control so as not to frighten her, but it has a will of its own. It fills and fills the longer I kiss her until it's fat and swollen, and I can't help that it's now pressed firmly against her soft rear end.

To my greatest surprise, my small Faela begins to *rub* herself against me. The tight ropes of my control slip and fracture as she moans under my mouth, and her perfect ass drags along me. My hands become even more eager, more bold, roaming down her thighs and up her belly, then under the sultry swell of her breasts. She does not flee, as I had feared—she leans even deeper into me, her body warming under my hands as her arousal takes her.

So my sad girl does have another side, a lush side, a side that thirsts for pleasure. I didn't expect her to be so sensual, but every movement I make, every press of my claws in her flesh, earns a whimper.

She is sensitive. Good.

I have not been a chaste god. That was never my purpose, never my intention. I enjoy all of life's bounties, delight in them, and find every opportunity to bask in the glow of desire. I have found joy in monks, in fairies, in strapping young men. Each carried their own flavor, their own unique aroma, and I appreciated all of them for what they were.

But none of them compare to what it feels like to twine myself around Faela. Her nipples brush across my chest as she breathes, and her delicate pussy caresses my cock with each of her unconscious movements. She simply radiates sex, as if it were baked into her blood, and the smell of it is roaring my name. I want to eat her, absorb her into myself, and never release her again.

Most certainly, she is my chosen one. The one picked for me from the thousands of years that have passed since my making.

Forty.

I startle myself out of my own licentious haze with the thought. My time with her is limited. This may be one of only a few moments I can share with her, and I would rather it be on a soft bed in a warm room than in a dirty river.

We can do the river thing later, once I've unlocked the feral, lusty animal inside her.

With Faela still wrapped around my hips, I get to my feet. She gasps at the shock of cool air above the water and peels her lips away from mine.

"Kireth...?" she asks, clasping me tight as if I might drop her.

I chuckle into her hair. "Hold on to me. I'm taking you home."

This earns a scandalized little gasp. "Like this?"

"Who will see us?" I ask, stepping out of the river, her butt resting pleasantly against my fully erect cock. "The sheep? I will remember that I'm being judged by sheep as we pass."

Faela covers her eyes with one arm, as if not seeing it herself will somehow hide her from the world, but doesn't ask to be put down as I carry her easily up the riverbank toward the collapsing farmhouse. I kick open the door and take the stairs two at a time, eager to lay my sopping wet mortal on her soft bed.

There, I will show her everything. All of life's mysteries will unravel before her eyes, including me.

Chapter Nine

FAELA

Oh, I have never felt a feeling so sinful as this. It is delightful. Sensational. I want Kireth touching every part of me, his hands teaching me the edges of my body, his mouth showing me how to play his tantalizing game.

I know for certain I want him inside of me. It is a primal feeling, an urging from down deep in my belly for that soft mushroom head to open me up so I can draw it into my depths. The channel between my legs is clenching and opening again, over and over, as that stiff cock runs across me while Kireth carries me up the stairs.

When we are safely inside my room, he lowers me to the bed. I release his neck and fall back onto the quilt where I am, to my surprise, not ashamed to have him see me—all of me.

He drags in a harsh breath as his eyes drink me up. His pupils are huge and dark, absorbing almost all the red.

Perhaps even his horns have grown, now longer and radiating out even farther from his head.

"You are beautiful," he says, voice barely more than a whisper, as he drags a talon down from my collarbone to my belly. "The loveliest creature I've ever seen."

I do not believe he's telling me a lie. No, by the look in his eyes, the way his tail curls with pleasure behind him, he has seen something divine appear and the only person in the room is me. It is baffling, that he would want me, a nothing of a girl.

"I've felt that way about you since the moment you appeared to me," I say, exposing everything I've been keeping locked up. But I feel I can trust him with these words now, the Kireth who went on a quest to help my little farm.

That mischievous grin returns, the one that plays at the corners of his mouth and hints at what else is to come. My god crouches over me, his knees trapping my hips, and brings one clawed hand up underneath my breast to gently tease my nipple. If I thought that felt marvelous, it doesn't compare to when he brings his head down and those perfect lips latch onto me. Against my will, my back arches, pushing my breast further into his mouth, and his cock surges where it prods at my thigh.

"A marvelous creature," Kireth whispers as he moves to pay attention to my other nipple. "So willing for me."

I am. I would do anything he asked if it meant he would keep unleashing this tumult of bliss across my body. While he licks and nips at my breasts, his hand ventures down until his claws are squeezing the thickest part of my thigh. I sense he is holding himself back for my pleasure, for my comfort, and I'm not sure I want him to.

I long to see the real Kireth, the true Kireth, hiding

underneath the exterior of a self-assured immortal. So I whimper his name, and he lifts his head from his attentions, a look of concern crossing his face.

"Did I hurt you?" he asks, brow furrowed. I didn't expect this considerate side to him.

"No." I shake my head forcefully. "I just..." How do I put to words what I want? I seek a fulfillment that only he can give me, something that will ease the growing heat between my legs. "I need you," is all I can think to say, and this time his smile is wide and whole and full of an emotion I can't quite place.

"Ah, yes," he says, kissing the valley between my breasts. "I understand."

I'm glad he does, but when he lowers himself so his head is over my hips, I'm not so sure anymore. I know that thick cock of his belongs inside me, and it doesn't look like he's about to grant my wish.

"Kireth?" I ask as he shifts us so he's crouched between my knees. He holds up a hand, and there's a *shhk!* sound as his claws withdraw.

I didn't know they could do that.

"Will you trust me?" he asks, running his now smooth fingertips up and down my thighs. I long for him to edge just a little closer, to find the curls at the juncture of my legs and dip underneath them.

"Of course," I say, because I do.

I gasp as his cool hand slides between my thighs and, with a gentle nudge, urges them apart. My legs obey immediately, widening enough that he sighs with satisfaction.

No one has ever seen me there, in my most vulnerable place, but what do I have to hide from an immortal being? One who has probably lain with thousands of others? I try not to let the jealousy rise in me, fierce and hot—but I'm distracted from it immediately by a gust of cool air on my sensitive skin as Kireth dips his head between my legs.

"Oh!" My pussy tightens and then releases again as he breathes on me, and there's a steady warmth building there as he peers up over my mound of curly hair.

He chuckles. "I haven't even touched you yet." He licks the tip of his index finger, sensually lapping at it with his pink tongue, wetting it until it's dripping. His eyes don't leave mine as he lowers it and softly runs it across my outer folds. I've touched myself there, of course, but it has not prepared me for the way he's caressing me, teasing just the ridges of me as a droplet of liquid seeps down.

"You're already so wet for me," he says with delicious approval. "I will make sure you are a sad girl no longer."

The pad of his finger slides down and I gasp, all my muscles curling up instinctively as he passes over the sensitive nub hidden there. It feels like pure light. Then he returns, and this time I'm prepared for the pleasure that barrels through me when he stops and swishes his fingertip back and forth. The light is expanding, becoming more and more blinding.

Kireth laughs at my wriggling. "Just like I thought. It won't take much." It seems he's had his fill of my clit, so he moves his fingers downward toward that starving place beneath it.

But then I feel something wet and hot on me, and I cry out when I realize an immortal demon is licking me between the legs.

My thighs squeeze together at the sudden spark of glory that shoots up through my body.

"Relax, lovely," he says, dropping his mouth again to that beautiful, incredible, wonderful spot. I try not to trap his head this time as that bountiful delight ripples through me, over and over as his tongue dances with my body the way it played with my tongue.

I understand much more now.

While he lazily laps at me, each pass making me writhe and moan, I feel Kireth shifting. Soon a finger prods at my opening, spreading around all the liquid gathered there. Then he presses it inside me.

Instinctually I draw back at the pressure, but he's insistent, holding my hips in place with one hand while he explores me with the other.

"It will feel good," he promises, nudging at me again. That spasming has returned, and I'm opening and closing while he continues licking me, harder and faster. After applying more pressure, the finger slips inside me, and oh, it feels like sunshine and warm breezes when it fills me up. My hips buck against his mouth, and Kireth chuckles.

"It will be so good making you come for me," he says, half to me and half to himself.

I don't know what he means, but now a pressure is growing right where his finger has begun thrusting inside me, where his tongue is tantalizing me endlessly. That blinding light swells and takes over my vision, and the nearly painful pressure suddenly releases, blowing me over with the force of it.

And is it joyous. I cry out as my god continues to shove that finger so marvelously into me, his tongue working at a feverish pace. In seconds, another sharp burst hits me, and I feel myself suddenly leaking.

Kireth groans, and his mouth sucks up everything.

"There we are," he murmurs, sitting upright. His eyes are hooded and full of a burning lust, so plain on his face that I would blush if I weren't already panting and hot. His cock is curved upward, the bright gray head underneath oozing some kind of white liquid.

I know exactly where I want that to go. But I reach out to it first, and Kireth's eyes widen.

"Oh?" He takes his cock in his hand and sits up so I can reach him better. "What do you think of it?"

"I want to know what it feels like."

He grins and urges me on.

My touch is hesitant at first, but when Kireth sucks in a sharp breath and tilts his head back, I grow more adventurous. I want to feel the full heft of it, the promise of it, to try to understand how this great big swollen thing will fit inside me. As I run my hand up and down, the skin over his cock's soft head moves, revealing even more light flesh. I lean down, and, as he did for me, brush my tongue over just the slit at the tip.

Kireth moans, and his hand finds my hair. "You must be kidding," he whispers to himself. "Faela, you are a goddess in your own right."

I continue exploring with my tongue, circling the head, watching his reactions. He tastes like the river with just a touch of salt. When I slip his cock between my lips, he groans and leans back on the bed. It is a marvel that I can do to him what he did for me as I swallow him up and then draw him back out again.

Abruptly, Kireth puts his hands on my shoulders and tugs me away.

"I'm not ready to go off yet," he says, his voice a little strangled. He has lost some of his composure, and I see a glimpse of the true, uncertain Kireth peering out. His arms wrap around me as he lowers me to the bed, kissing my nose, staring into me with his bright red eyes.

"I want to take you all the way there," he says in a low, rasping voice. "Will you come with me?"

I don't have to think before I respond. "Yes. I will."

It's all he needs. My god reaches down between my thighs once more and runs his fingers through my slickness like a sled over a snowy hill. He puts one fingertip inside me, and I gasp underneath him until suddenly, there are two. I fall still as the second one starts to work its way through my tight entrance.

It is too much. I can't take it.

"You need to be prepared for me," Kireth explains, using my stored-up liquid to ease his way in. I gasp and tighten as they wriggle in deeper, pushing me apart, and my body aches underneath it as much as it demands more.

Once inside, Kireth pets me with both fingers in unison. I'm stretching wide for him, but gladly, eagerly, ready to arrive wherever he's taking me. It could be hours or mere seconds that go by as he increases his speed, forcing my channel to shift and widen and accept him, leading me back to that place where I'm writhing and moaning with unspent energy. When I'm so slippery and spread out that his fingers move freely, he withdraws them. I whine, missing the feel of them.

"Soon," he murmurs.

Kireth's horns glimmer in the lamplight as he kneels between my legs, pushing his cock down toward the space that now feels so empty, my thighs spread around his hips. He slips through my inner folds, brushing himself over my sensitive clit.

"It might not feel good at first," he says, pausing to run his hands up and down my hips, over my belly to my pelvis, tangling his fingers in the hair there. "But I promise it will."

The moment that wide, soft head finds me, there's

suddenly a pressure up against my small slit. I know what he means now. And yet I'm so wet, so slippery, that the tip of his cock manages to fit through, stretching me almost to the point I think I might break. It's uncomfortable and tense, like he warned me, and yet still so erotic.

"Kireth..."

His name falls from my lips, and he gets a sinful smile. He pauses his invasion and instead, draws back, tracing my edges with the head of his cock and urging my tight opening to soften for him. Then he tries again, demanding I allow him through. My body is weeping, lathering him up, and this time, he slips inside. My muscles tense as I open wide for him, and it burns in a new, shocking way.

"Breathe," my god tells me, dropping onto his elbows so he can be closer to my face. He kisses both my cheeks, and then my mouth, just stroking that malleable, sweet cockhead in and out until I'm bucking under him. Every pass triggers a burst of color behind my eyes, even as it aches. That familiar sweet tenseness builds in my abdomen, and I wonder if I might simply blow apart.

Then his cock slides further in, spreading me even more, and I gasp as my channel swallows him. There's a wire-tight tension between my legs as he gently slips deeper and deeper with each small thrust of his hips. It hurts, stretched as wide as I am, but somehow it's wonderful, too.

"There we are, my girl," Kireth croons, pushing my hair away from my sweat-slicked forehead. "Swallow me up."

And I do. Every bone in my body is begging for more and he gives it to me, sliding all the way in at last. I cringe as the tightness becomes almost unbearable. Kireth stops and exhales a long, relieved breath.

"There we are." He drops his forehead to mine, framing my face with his hands. He kisses me, again and again, until

I sense my muscles starting to relax. That terrible tightness fades, and soon all I want is for his perfect, satisfying cock to do more. I don't know what it is exactly that I desire, but I need it—now.

Slowly, Kireth withdraws, and immediately I'm begging to be filled again. I don't realize that I'm whimpering until he buries himself inside me, cutting me off. It's tight and uncomfortable and yet so delicious that I need him to keep going. It's as if my need is speaking directly to him, because he repeats the motion, filling and withdrawing, sliding easily through my wetness.

I moan his name, wrapping my arms around him, tugging him closer to me, desiring only his body against mine. He chuckles and presses his face into my hair as he strokes in and out, his chest weighing me down, and the discomfort fades into a blistering pleasure.

Somewhere deep inside me, that same sweet sensation is swelling upward, and each time he thrusts, it stacks higher and higher, like a steep set of stairs leading me toward an unknown destination. I wrap my legs around his waist to draw him in even further, if that were possible, as my hips rise to meet each of his movements. My nose is buried in his neck, inhaling his warm smell.

"Fuck," Kireth whispers, his arms curling around me. "You feel wonderful, Faela. Like stars and sugar."

I'm pleased to know that he, too, feels this unimaginable wonder, and he picks up his speed, plunging in and out while the steps appear quicker and quicker in front of me. Soon I'm running up them, crying out as he digs even deeper. His cock's soft head brushes past something inside me that sends a lightning bolt across my body, and I feel tears prick at the corners of my eyes. I can barely stand it, as if I might simply explode underneath him.

"Let it take you," he says into my ear. "Give in to me, and to your pleasure."

I obey. My body squeezes so tight it's almost painful, and now I'm at the very top of the stairs, ready to careen over the edge. That's when everything releases at once.

I'm blinded by it, deafened by it, completely overtaken by it. I hear Kireth groan as he pushes through my powerful clenching, slamming into me over and over, and my whole body rocks with the force of my rapture.

"Kireth!" My voice is broken and ragged. He shoves inside me one last time, as deep as he can get, and his cock swells up thick and fat. I'm crying now, clutching him as close as I can as he draws out this indescribable joy. Then he bursts, and hot liquid shoots against my deepest, most sensitive place.

I crumble and melt into nothing.

Kireth nearly collapses on top of me, holding himself up with one hand as I shake like a leaf underneath him. He kisses me deeply and fully. I've seen him, the real him, and it is a vision like none other. I've found something beautiful, something priceless, and I clutch him as close to me as I can.

Chapter Ten

KIRETH

My Faela. So tight and warm and wonderful. Every one of her little mewls, her moans and her cries, has refilled a reservoir in me that I thought was empty. I bring her as close to me as I can, reveling in her scent, in the soft clench of her body, in the way her eyelashes flutter closed as she basks in the warm glow of our pleasure.

I have lain with many mortals, and even other immortals, but nothing compares to this. I never want to leave her side again.

The force with which this desire hits me is catastrophic. *Forty*. That is all I have left with my sweet, perfect farm girl. I do not get to have her forever. Never before has the weight of my immortality, of my obligation, settled so heavy and claustrophobic on my shoulders.

I stay inside her as long as I can, simply reveling in our togetherness. What has this woman done to me? I want to be joined to her this way for eternity, sunk in her flawless depths.

"Kireth?" her tiny voice says, and I relish the way she says my name.

I stroke her hair, which is still wet from the river. "Yes, sweet girl?"

"That was amazing." She nuzzles deeper into the hollow of my throat. "Whatever we just did, I won't forget it as long as I live."

I can hear the words she isn't saying. She knows I will have to leave, too. Even then, she doesn't regret it. I hope she will still feel the same way when I'm gone. Perhaps she will find a husband or wife of her own, and give them the impossible, heady pleasure she gave me.

My stomach roils with jealousy at the idea of anyone else having my sweet Faela, and it is a strange and unfamiliar feeling. I want to be the only creature to know her this way, to love her as she deserves.

I almost don't notice it as I think it. *Love.* Is that what this feeling is, to want so deeply for her happiness, to see in her all my needs and desires fulfilled? I've heard of it, listened to songs and read poems about it, but never really understood it until now. My past affairs have been merely that, sating a need, pursuing beauty, or simply enjoying the world and all the blessings in it.

Perhaps the curse the oracle put on me was not meant to kill the farm. Perhaps it was meant to hurt me in an even deeper way, by making me fall in love with a mortal—and then taking her from me.

"I will never forget you, either," I tell her, my cock finally slipping free as I bring her closer to my body. Belatedly, I hope that I have not put a child in her. Then leaving her would be an even more tortuous fate.

We will have to do something about that in the future. I vow to keep a close eye on her the next two weeks and taste her often until I'm certain I haven't planted a seed in her.

Twist my arm.

When the sun is fully down and Faela's breaths have gone quiet and steady, I give myself over to sleep.

THE NEXT MORNING, she is up much earlier than I am, as is usual. I wake up long enough to notice that she's freeing herself from my embrace, tugging off my arm and unwinding my tail from around her thigh. It thumps unhappily as she departs the bed, and I pull her quilt close to me instead because it smells like her.

When I'm finally up—my body had a lot of magic to recover after using up so much of it on my quest—the sun is shining and the world feels like a new and wondrous place.

Outside, Faela is laboring over the animals.

"Sweet girl?" I call out, and she shoots to her feet like a marionette on a string. She hikes up her dress and jogs over to me, then freely flings her arms around my waist as if she's been waiting a long time to do that.

I knew she had this side to her. Underneath all that misery and death, there was an affectionate, passionate woman waiting to be let out.

"I'm glad you're up," she says. "Look."

When we've finally disentangled, her pointed finger draws my eyes up to the fields. There are patches of green among all the dying plants. Some of them have recovered, as if time was rewound.

I gather her up close again and breathe in deeply. It looks like my mother did intend to help me, after all.

"What can I do today?" I ask.

Faela hesitates, clearly afraid of using more tasks—especially now that we have crossed this boundary between us.

"Can you water and tend the plants?" she asks hopefully.

I nod in agreement. I will happily do this for her.

My farm girl clasps my hands in hers and kisses me on the cheek. "Thank you."

I bound away to do my work, looking forward to when we're finished and the sun is setting once more.

FAELA

That afternoon, Kireth hunts down some ingredients to make another potion, one he asks me not so politely to drink.

"I saw what went in there!" It was altogether foul. I cover my mouth with one hand to prevent it from even getting near me. "I will not!"

He puts a hand on his hip, annoyed at my rebelliousness.

"This is important. We must make sure I don't plant a half-immortal in you." Then he unties the string of his loincloth, letting it fall down and revealing all of him, every last delectable inch of him.

"That's the price," he says, staring at me as his blood starts to flow down, causing his cock to slowly thicken and rise. The moment I see it, I want it, so I reach in his direction—but Kireth shakes the bowl in front of me again. "Nuh-uh. Not until you drink it."

Finally I give in, and try to guzzle it all down before my stomach can revolt. I gag a few times, working my hardest to keep the terrible liquid in my belly. My god pats my back to comfort me, but I know he's a little amused, too. When I'm finished and I don't think I'll throw it all up, he hefts me into his arms and carries me upstairs.

The droplets of rejuvenating potion are indeed working. It's slow, but the black mold has begun to drain out of the soil, as if the filthy film covering everything is now being pried away. For the crops that have recovered, Kireth uses his magic to foster their growth.

"The good soil helps," he says, flexing his arm for me as if to show off just how powerful he is. "And my well refills much more rapidly now."

Apparently, having the world's most incredible sex does wonders for his reserve of magic. He is always keen to use it, ready to show off how wielding his cock like a weapon of bliss has made him stronger.

Kireth likes to torture me. After plundering me with his tongue and fingering me until I come all over him, his favorite thing is to lay me face down on the bed, fully supine, and then hold himself up on top of me so his cock is nudging between the cheeks of my rear. I widen my legs just enough that he can taste me, and instantly all that delicious heat is surging downward, readying me for him.

That's the worst part—how eager my body will be while he simply continues to tease, the head of his cock rubbing urgently against my clit and just barely dipping inside me. He likes to repeat this until I'm begging, my pussy weeping with need, and then he slides himself in where he belongs.

My immortal is creative, I will give him that. When we are bathing in the river, he brings me into his lap like the first time we kissed and guides his cock easily inside me. He lifts my hips and lowers them again, showing me how I can decide our speed and depth.

Now it is my turn to torture him.

I relish this new power, and when I focus hard on the places our bodies connect, I can pinpoint what makes both of us moan.

"Use me," Kireth growls as I sink deep and then rise quickly, and the next time, I only take in half of him. "I want you to come over and over on my cock. I want you to drench me."

And oh, how my body listens when he talks to me that way. When I find just what it wants, just what it needs, I seek out my gratification single-mindedly. Kireth groans in my arms, his claws squeezing my ass because he knows I like it when he handles me roughly.

"Yes," he says through gritted teeth. "Find it, sweet girl. I want to hear your pretty voice."

At his request, I chase after that blistering wonder, that powerful shock of sensation that comes whenever I take him halfway deep and his cockhead rubs against the inside of me. I soon learn where it feels best, and then I ride him, the contortions of his face mimicking my own as we both run headlong for our finishes. When I come around him, I'm crying out his name, and he buries himself deep as he shoots his hot seed inside me. It is the most exquisite feeling I've ever experienced to be so completely sated, collapsing against Kireth while the river flows around us.

There is one terrible side to all of this: knowing that he will, eventually, leave me.

Yet we easily fall into a pattern. He cares for the plants

and I care for the livestock, and in the evening—before we retire for our nightly activities—we repair what's fallen apart and broken over the years. I've sold off the wool for a new window and a big pile of good wood for replacing fences, with enough left over to buy us fruit and bread and even some treats. People in the village are surprised to see me selling cheese at the little stall Kireth built for me, which Ryc pulls into town each week.

I'm the girl with the cursed farm, and at first, they are reluctant to buy from me. Perhaps my cheese is cursed, too, they whisper. But Kireth has imbued it with some of his delicious magic, and soon they are buying me out of stock whenever I come to the village to sell.

It seems that perhaps my luck has turned around.

Chapter Eleven

KIRETH

Nothing has ever felt so right or so good as this life. Every day I work in the field, and while once upon a time I found such a thing danger-ously tedious, doing it for Faela puts a spring in my step and guides my hands as I care for the crops. Every evening, I enjoy her body, making her moan and whimper, cry and scream. She holds on to my horns while she rides my cock and crumples to the bed while I take her from behind. She's so tight and wet that every stroke makes an indecent noise. The flawless, tight grip of her cunt sends me flying over the cliff so hard and so fast that I worry I might plummet to my death.

Nothing has ever felt so right or so good as loving my farm girl.

I've stopped counting the tasks, and I don't know if Faela has noticed yet. She is absorbed, understandably so, in the recovery of her beloved farm. The grass grows thicker and greener than ever, and now her cows and sheep are fattening up, giving us more milk. Meat will be plentiful this fall.

If I do not count them, then our time together can never run out. Now that I have her, there is no possible way I could leave.

The crops are coming back to life and thriving thanks to the potion, my magic, and the mighty power of the sun. It somewhat assuages my guilt for my part in all of this to see the farm coming back to life. We spend a few days digging new irrigation to make sure the plants get plenty of water, and soon we will begin harvesting the leafy greens.

Every day that we use the potion, the curse retreats farther. We are pushing it away from the house and toward the riverbank, and that's where we plan to capture it. Faela has an old jewelry box where her mother kept a single silver chain, and it will work perfectly for our purposes. When the curse is finally small and weak enough to be caught, we will trap it inside, lock it, and throw away the key.

Well, metaphorically speaking. I have advised her we should keep it in the event she makes a terrible enemy one day and wants to wreak havoc upon them.

"That's an awful thing to do," she says, but she's laughing merrily as she says it. "You are such a troublemaker."

Then the day comes that the curse has been whittled down to a small black globule, occupying a square foot of land just to the northeast of the house. I call for Faela to bring the box, and we both crouch on either side of the shivering patch of darkened earth. I torment one edge with a droplet of the potion, and the curse skirts away—heading right toward the box.

"Open it!" I call out. Faela lifts the lid as I drop more potion, driving the curse toward her. At that moment, I wonder if this was a mistake, and it ought to be me holding the box in case the curse tries to attack. Then, at least, it would land on me, and I might have a chance of fighting it off. I don't know what it would do if it latched onto Faela.

One more drop, and the blob leaps off the ground, ready to run for it. Faela jumps to attention and tilts the open box down... scooping up the curse inside.

She slams the lid, pushes down the latch, and twists the key in the lock. The box clicks with a rather satisfactory sound.

Now the pox on her farm has been removed, and it thrashes and wails from inside its wooden prison. The deed is done.

When we take the box inside and set it on the mantel over the fire, I congratulate Faela on such a marvelous job trapping that wretched thing. She acted quickly and decisively, and I am proud of her.

"We still ought to get rid of it," she says, eyeing the box warily. "Anyway, I have a surprise to celebrate!"

She practically runs to the cellar to retrieve her prize. When she returns, she's carrying two big water skins. I watch with curiosity, my damned tail flicking wildly in anticipation. She pours the liquid in the skin into a cup, and I'm overtaken by the marvelous scent of wine.

Oh, and it is sweet, as sweet as my girl's cunt. My mouth is watering by the time she hands me the cup.

"You're quiet," she says, appearing a little nervous. "I thought you liked wine?"

"I don't like wine," I tell her, taking it from her hand like it is a fragile baby rabbit. "I *love* it."

I drain the cup in a few quick gulps, relishing the way the wine slides down my tongue and into my belly, where it begins warming me from the inside out.

Clearly pleased by my reaction, Faela pours a cup of her own and sips it slowly and pointedly. Right. Wine is for enjoying at a more reasonable speed. But the taste reminds me of a time long past, when I enjoyed the company of other immortals and half-immortals, and we had great, wondrous orgies in the hall of the gods.

Faela and I sit outside that night, lying in the lush green grass with her legs sprawled across mine. We each take a sip of wine now and then, and there's a pleasant, buzzing haze descending on me.

"Kireth?" she asks, and I realize neither of us has spoken in a while. I wonder what she's thinking about.

"Mmhmm?" I could lie in this spot, having wine with my sweet girl, until the end of time.

"Do you know why that curse was here?" she asks, and sits up a little. "I've always wondered what you did when you left and came back with the potion."

Oh. That. If there was anything I'd rather less think about.

I'm not sure how much to tell her. Outright lying feels wrong—not to my good Faela. But there are many undignified points in the story on my part. Ultimately, what happened here is my fault, isn't it?

The death of her mother. The struggle and the strife on the farm.

That's an ugly thought, to know I am to blame for all this. What would my sweet girl do if she learned the truth? She would be devastated. She might even dismiss me and send me back to my temple.

I can't have that.

"I went and saw my mother," I confess. I slide closer to her, bringing her head onto my chest so she's using me as a pillow and I can play with her hair while I drink more wine.

Faela tilts her chin up to look at me. "Your mother? Who is that?"

"The goddess Lucia. Well, 'mother' is the best approximation of our relationship." I snort. She was really a terrible mother in that sense of the word.

"Wait, the goddess? She gave birth to you?"

Again I laugh. Talking with mortals about the affairs of gods has always amused me because they are so certain that their experience is universal.

"She made me," I explain, and go on to tell her how Lucia carved me from stone fully formed and breathed life into my lungs.

"So you've always been this way?" Faela asks.

It depends on whether she means in body or in mind. Certainly nothing has changed on the outside, but I feel as if the interior Kireth I am now is nowhere near the one I was only a few months ago. I have discovered a whole new plane of existence here, separate from either the mortal or the immortal one.

Instead, I just nod. "Always."

"Hmm," she says, and returns to lying back against me. "So Lucia decided to help us?"

"She recognized the curse when I described it and gave me the recipe."

"That was very kind of her," Faela says, and there's a little twinge in her voice like she senses there are some words missing. "I didn't realize that gods were so selfless."

"We are mother and son," I say by way of explanation. "More wine?" I am eager to change the subject.

Faela hands me her cup without a word and falls back on the grass to look up at the stars as I fetch us refills. We consume more and more of the delicious nectar until we are rolled up together and giggling, and I'm kissing her face all over. She wails with protest as she laughs, trying to escape.

"Just stop being kissable," I say accusingly, my voice slurring.

"I'm trying, I'm trying!" Her body is rubbing so deliciously at my groin that I might just pop off right here. I pull her against me and peel up the skirt of her dress, where I find she's wearing nothing underneath.

"Oh, you minx!" I reach down and grip her soft, pretty hips. She thrusts them into me, and with all that heady wine bubbling up inside me, I only want one thing.

I test her first, winding a finger down between her legs. Usually I fuck her with my mouth first, cock second, but tonight is different. We have finally conquered the menace that kept this wonderful, hard-working girl locked up. I need to feel her wrapped all the way around me, the only sound on the farm her colorful moans.

Faela gasps as I push a finger inside her, and she's already soaked for me. I wonder how long she's been lusting already.

In one motion, I roll on top of her, and my hips easily find their place between her legs. I hike up her ass with my hands because I plan on fucking her hard and deep. Her eyes are wide, her lips spread in a circle. When she says my name, there's a fervent need in her drunken voice.

"Please, Kireth," she says, her hazel eyes bright under the starlight.

Of course I acquiesce, positioning the head of my cock right at that small, pinkish slit. It gasps for me, opening and closing as her body thrums with her desire. I need to fill her and become filled with her.

Faela is so wet that it's easy to plunge into her, and she writhes underneath me. I fuck her like this, burying myself so deep that my sac slaps against her fine, round ass until she's tearing out grass with her hands and her head is thrashing back and forth.

"Kireth," she moans. "You feel so good, I might die. Please, please—" She descends into nonsense as I reach as far into her as I can and pump there, searching out the place that drives her wild.

Almost immediately her climax takes her, and Faela screams as her head falls back and her cunt grips like a vise around me. Oh, yes, this is definitely my purpose for existing.

I pour all of myself into her, knowing that she is drinking the remedy I make every week. Each thrust tears more of my own orgasm out of me, and it's beyond anything I've had in my long, long lifetime.

I struggle not to simply collapse on top of her. Instead I roll us over, my cock still engorged inside her, and press her forehead to my chest.

Faela traces the patterns on my body with the pad of her finger, as if she enjoys the feel of my skin. It is a wondrous thing to be loved by this woman.

"I'm so glad that terrible curse is gone," I murmur against her hair, inhaling the sweet scent of it, of *her*. The wine is working its way through me, and I think how all that matters to me now is her happiness. "I'm sorry for my part in it."

Faela's body stiffens in my arms.

"What?" she asks quietly. "What do you mean, Kireth?"

My mouth closes so hard my teeth clack together. What have I done?

Chapter Twelve

FAELA

I knew he wasn't telling me something. My trickster god isn't nearly as clever as he thinks he is, not anymore. I've learned his tells, like the way his tail weaves pinched little patterns in the air when he's thinking about lying, or how he worries his lip with one of his canines when he won't say what he's thinking. His voice changes, somewhat higher pitched, when he's not telling the full truth.

I sit up quickly, pushing my dress down to cover myself. I repeat my words.

"What do you mean by 'your part,' Kireth?"

He flinches when I use his name. He bites his lip and doesn't look at me, and I know he's hiding something. Something important.

"Did you really have something to do with the curse?" I press.

"Maybe?" He forces a smile and holds up two fingers just an inch apart. "Just a little bit."

How is that possible? The sickness befell the farm long before I called on him.

"I don't understand." When Kireth reaches for my thigh, I pull it away. "Tell me the whole truth."

Sighing, he rights himself and crosses his legs under him.

"I'm not a very good person, you know." He gives me a rueful smile, trying to lighten the mood. "Not since the day Lucia made me."

I know all of this. I witnessed it firsthand—though he has changed as time has gone on.

"So?" I'm not going to let him get away without explaining himself.

"So..." Kireth trails off, his tail lashing behind him. "I, um, might have gotten on the bad side of an oracle." He flinches at his own words.

"What did you do?" I'm trying to control the heat rising into my cheeks, but I must try not to judge him until I hear the whole story. There's no possible way he's responsible for what happened here, right?

Kireth doesn't look at me as he talks. "I was summoned, once upon a time. Hundreds of years ago. My master at the time sent me on a ridiculous quest, and I was looking for a way to, um..." He trails off. "I needed to punish him for it. So I went to the oracle to ask what his future was."

"Why?" I ask.

"I wanted to know what his life would be like. If he would have a family or children."

I feel cold, but I don't speak. After a long breath, Kireth continues.

"I stole a goat and traded it to the oracle for the answer. But she said that I couldn't interfere with the future she told or there would be repercussions."

That coldness spreads down my arms and legs. Kireth reaches out to take my hands, but I bring them back to my chest. His shoulders sag.

"When I found out he would meet a woman in a nearby town and marry her in just two months' time…" His eyes finally rise to mine and they are frightened. I don't think I've ever seen my god look afraid before.

"Tell me the rest of the story," I say, my voice hard. It's as if I'm watching a huge, terrible boulder rolling downhill toward the village.

Kireth's voice pitches higher as he continues, his shame growing. "She said if I got in the way of the man's destiny, she would ruin me in kind—in proportion to my error.

"I didn't listen. When I returned from my quest, it was right at the perfect moment. On the day my master was supposed to meet his future wife, I broke his wagon so he couldn't leave the way he was intended to."

It's as if my blood has stopped moving through my veins. "So she ruined you in kind," I whisper.

Kireth nods slowly. "That is what Lucia said. That the curse on your farm was my punishment."

The world tilts, and I struggle to stay upright.

"My mother." The words are strangled as they come out of me, because they are so hard to say. To even think. "My mother died because of that curse."

Kireth's eyes plead with mine. "I didn't know, Faela. Truly, I didn't."

Why me? Why *her*? I feel that there's more, and as deep as the wound already is, he has not yet told me everything.

"Kireth." I say his name again, slowly, the tears streaming hot and fast from my eyes as the love that I felt for this demon in front of me morphs into something painful and ugly. "Why did the oracle choose my farm?"

"Faela, please." He grabs my hands in his and holds them, even as I try to get away. "Listen to me. I couldn't have known that I would ever find you—"

"Stop!" I've never shouted at him before, and Kireth leans back in surprise, releasing me. I get to my feet and dust myself off, trying to hide how my hands are shaking. "You didn't answer me. Why my farm? I know that you know!"

His eyes are impossibly sad as he searches my face, clearly hoping for a way out. But when I offer none, he lowers his eyes and speaks.

"The oracle saw the future. She realized the best way to hurt me was through you. That the curse would bring me to you, and..." My pain rises inside me like a beast. "...I would fall in love with you, and then, by the nature of my agreement, I would be forced to leave you."

He loves me. He loves me, and I am his punishment. I was just an object to be used, a pawn to inflict on him what he inflicted upon someone else hundreds of years ago.

I can't look at Kireth's miserable face any longer, so I turn and rush into the house.

"Faela!" he calls out. "Wait, farm girl, please—"

The door slams closed behind me.

My misery has no bottom. It is a well yawning wide underneath me, sucking me toward it, threatening to swallow me into the nothingness.

All of this was because of *him*.

It's as if something has opened inside of me, and a black curse in my own locked chest is streaming out. I scream in rage, thinking of how this all could have been prevented, how my mother could still be alive if Kireth weren't so foolish and troublesome. Blazing hot, I pick up a chair that we repaired together last week and throw it. It strikes the wall, splintering, and falls to the floor in a pile of sticks.

I sink to my knees and realize that I'm drenched between the thighs after our roll in the grass, and I scream again, tearing pieces of cloth out of my dress so I can clean myself up. I pour more wine, and more wine, guzzling all of it until I stumble up the steps to our bed.

This is the place where we've slept every night and made love innumerable times in the last few months.

Months. It's been so long, surely we should have run out of tasks by now. Surely I've used all forty of them.

And then I realize: he stopped counting.

The splinter digging into my chest becomes sharper, more acute. Who knows how many tasks Kireth did for me without counting a single one of them? Was his plan to stay here forever?

My pain is a river and I am trapped in it, flailing, trying desperately to grab onto a root or a rock so I can stop being dragged away. I fall into the bed and sob, remembering how Mother would always come and kiss me before bed, even once I was a fully grown woman.

Little girls never grow out of their mother's kisses, she'd said.

I bring up the quilt to my face. It smells like Kireth: dense woods and undergrowth, fresh rivers, a new sprout coming out of the ground.

He lied because he knew the truth was too much for my love to survive. And perhaps it is.

KIRETH

The front door of the house slams closed, and I know I am no longer welcome in Faela's home.

It is hers, after all. It was never mine. I slept there, and fixed what I could, and ate dinner there because it made her happy. But a mortal's home is not meant for me. I was always intended to be a temporary presence there.

Fresh hay bales are waiting inside the barn. I lie down on them and curl up because it's starting to get cooler at night. I think of Faela's soft bed, the scent of her everywhere, ensconcing me in its comforting glow. I remember drawing her into me, tucking her head under my chin, wrapping my tail around her thigh where it lay between my legs as we fell asleep.

She will never forgive me.

Up at the house, I hear an immense *crack!*, like something large has broken into pieces. She screams with fury, and I think I underestimated the lion lying dormant inside her.

I am a truly miserable thing, to have brought this upon her.

The noise ceases after some time, and then the candles in the windows are extinguished. I watch the house through the open barn door as Faela goes to bed without me.

How can I possibly undo what I've done? When my actions created so much heartache and misery, and stole so much from her?

"Overstayed your welcome, have you?"

Lucia's voice startles me enough that I tumble off the hay bale. The great goddess chuckles from where she stands stooped under the low barn ceiling. She snaps her fingers, and slowly her body shrinks until she's a much more manageable seven or eight feet tall.

"You have always landed on your feet before, haven't you?" she says, stroking her chin thoughtfully. "This time... not so much."

I dust myself off. "She'll forgive me," I say with confidence so that perhaps, I'll believe it. But I'm not sure she will.

My mother simply shrugs. "It doesn't matter, unfortunately for you." She leans down close and smiles wickedly. "You're done here, Kireth. You have been for some time."

I balk. "But I wasn't counting my tasks!"

"Just because *you* weren't counting doesn't mean no one was counting." She narrows her sharp blue eyes. "Those were the rules when you were created. You have broken them by not returning to your temple when the time was up."

I chuckle uneasily. "The time can't be up yet, though." Have I done forty tasks since I stopped keeping track?

Lucia keeps a level gaze on me as she crosses her arms. "It is. You're done, Kireth."

I sprint to the door of the barn and throw it open. I can't go, not yet. I have to say goodbye to my sweet farm girl. My chosen one.

I take off at a run toward the house, but my feet won't move. They're trapped in mid-air, tethered by vines around my ankles.

With a yelp, I fall to the ground.

"Faela!" I shout. "Faela!"

But the house is silent as my mother slowly walks around me, examining me.

"You really love her." She chuckles, and it's a menacing sound. "I would never have guessed."

My Faela. I can't leave her—at least not without seeing her one more time. Not without telling her where I've gone.

"What if I do?" I snap, trying to unwind the vines. But they keep growing, tightening as they crawl up my body, trapping my tail to the ground. "So what if I've stayed? I'm immortal! The humans are forgetting us anyway. We don't serve a purpose!"

Lucia tilts her head thoughtfully. "You're right. She is likely the last one to ever summon you." Crouching in front of me, my mother tilts up my chin, and her pale face is decorated with a pitying smile. "You think you should get to stay, do you, even though you've broken all the rules? Even though she doesn't want you anymore?"

I don't care if she doesn't want me. I will live in this dark, stinky barn, and work the fields, and milk the cows for as long as I must to earn her love back. The idea of never having my farm girl again blots out all the light in the sky.

"Haven't I served long enough?" I twist away from her, but the vines are starting to wind around my arms now. "Haven't I earned the right to stay while the world forgets about me?"

Lucia chuckles. "That's not how this works, and you know it, Kireth." She rolls her shoulders, preparing for something, and I know now that I have not swayed her. "Since you are so insistent that you are now without purpose, perhaps it is time for you to join the others in oblivion."

Panic sweeps through me. "No," I whisper. "You can't mean to send me there."

"I do. That is your punishment for flagrantly abandoning your post and your duties." She raises her hands up in the air. "A fitting end for such an arrogant, spiteful child as you."

"You can't!" I scream as the vines squeeze around me, pulling me into the gaping hole in the ground. "You made me this way!" They cover my face, my throat, but still I cry, "Faela!" one last time.

My shout is swallowed up as the vines finally pull me under.

Chapter Thirteen

FAELA

"*Faela!*"

I wake up with a start at the sound of Kireth's screams. I drag myself out of bed, the wine pounding in my head, and run to the window. Whatever is happening out there, he's terrified. Worry creeps into my foggy mind.

Regardless of anything else, if he's in trouble, I have to help him.

Outside the window stands a great woman, pale and tall, wearing a white gown that reflects the moonlight so brightly she looks like pure silver.

Lucia. The goddess of the earth.

I rush down the stairs and out the front door as fast as my legs will move. Lucia stands in front of the barn, her hands raised to the sky. There is a hole in the ground in front of her, crawling with green vines.

"Kireth?" I call out. He doesn't answer. That can't be a good thing. "Where are you?"

"He's gone," the goddess says. She turns to me and lowers her arms, a gentle smile on her face that belies something much meaner. "Isn't that what you wanted, mortal?"

My head swims. Gone? He can't be gone. I was angry, yes—so angry, and heartbroken, and vengeful—but I didn't want him to leave.

"He left me?" I stumble forward. "He couldn't have."

"It was not by choice," Lucia says with a feminine giggle. "But he broke his rules, the promise of his existence, to stay with you longer. And so, he has been punished."

It is a bolt of lightning directly to my heart.

"No. You didn't." It can't be. I turn accusing eyes on her. "Why did you take him?"

She has a haughty look on her face. "It was past time."

"But he had tasks left to complete. He wasn't finished here!"

Lucia lets out a bored sigh. "He was finished. He had been, for a long time." She peers down at me, and she's tall, too tall. Unnaturally tall.

My stomach lurches. I knew he had stopped telling me when I used up one of my tasks. Despite that, were they still ticking away?

"And so this was his punishment?" I reach into the vines, searching for him, ripping off leaves and small branches trying to get him back out. The thorns bite into my flesh, but still I yank and pull.

"Stop, mortal." Lucia's voice is commanding, final. "He is not there. Not anymore."

I get up and stagger over to her. I don't care how tall she is, because I am angry.

"Then where is he?" I ask, my voice growing higher and louder. "Where is Kireth?"

"What do you care?" Lucia scoffs. "You were finished with him anyway."

Was I? Oh, he had hurt me. He had cut me as deep as one possibly could with his foolishness, his mischievous mistakes. But I don't know if I can ever truly be finished with the creature who hopped away like a puppy to do his chores, who took me so sweetly every night, and loved me so thoroughly. His devious little nature had carried a heavy price, but was it his fault that he had fallen in love with me, and I with him—and that's what made me the perfect target? He couldn't have known, it's true. He said it, but I didn't want to believe it, because I needed someone to blame for Mother's death.

"No. I wasn't finished. I'll never be finished." I grab a fistful of the goddess's dress in my hands, gripping it tightly, and she blinks down at me in surprise. "Where did you take him?"

"So rude when faced with a god," she says, shoving me away. "Perhaps the two of you are more alike than I thought."

I can't lose Kireth. Not now, after losing Mother. I need him here.

"Take me to him!" I demand.

The goddess tilts her head. "So angry. If you wanted him that much, you should have just said so." She wags a finger in my face. "But it's not so easy as just going to him. He is in the realm of forgotten gods now. Oblivion."

"Then bring him back!" I brush away stinging, angry tears. "I know you can!"

"I cannot. That place is beyond even my reach, unless I want to find myself banished there, too." But then Lucia pauses and taps her chin. "Perhaps you could retrieve him, though. Mortals are not so afflicted."

A spark of hope bursts in me. "How?"

I will do it. I need him here, with me, because I love him. Faced with his absence in my life forever, I know the truth. Whatever sins he's committed in the past, I'll do anything to bring him back.

"You will have to die." The goddess smiles sweetly. "Then you could pass through the barrier to the world beyond."

That spark of hope sizzles into nothing. Dying? That's the only way to see him again? But I cannot fathom it, not after watching Mother fade away. I can't go to that dark place and leave the farm behind. And what would be the point if we can never live our lives together?

"It's not permanent," Lucia says, watching my face with a smug smile.

Could I possibly trust another god? It might be a trap, and I'd simply die and remain that way.

"How do I know?" I ask, my eyebrows knitting in suspicion. "How do I know I'll come back to life?"

She shrugs. "I suppose that you don't. But I promise that if you succeed, if you can surmount the obstacles you'll face in reaching him, you will return to the world of the living."

Obstacles? I wonder what trials Lucia has planned for me on the other side.

"Time is ticking," she says, tapping the air. "Will you take my offer or not?"

Do I have a choice? Kireth saved my farm—he saved *me*. Now I have to save him.

"Fine," I say, holding out my hand. "Show me how to get there."

My last thought as I take the goddess's hand is that I hope Petal and Rye will be all right if I don't come back.

The moment my palm wraps around hers, a terrible pain shoots through me, straight down the middle as if it's trying to split me in half. I shriek and fall to the ground in agony.

"Dying is an ugly business," Lucia says, watching me with pity. "I suppose I should have warned you."

The stars overhead swim, blending with the moon in a swirl of bright light. My body crumples, and everything goes dark.

❧

KIRETH

When the doors open for me, I'm greeted by laughing voices and bright light. This yawning ceiling, these great marble walls, are all familiar to me. Walking in is like putting on an old coat.

They are all here. My old friends, my fellow long-gone immortals. They drink wine, and play merry card games, and fornicate in the corners—or in some cases, in large groups on one of the big beds above the mezzanine.

I am back home, in the hall of the gods.

But why?

"Kireth!" Anoinda rushes down the steps, naked. It's clearly just reached her ears that I've arrived. She throws her arms around me. "Ah, you mischievous little imp. I have been wondering when you might show up." She teases her hands down my chest to the tie of my loincloth.

My mind feels hazy, like everything is coated in a layer of cobwebs. But why am I here, now, in the home of the immortals? I haven't been here for many centuries, and...

The cobwebs get thicker, more impassable. I can't

remember what came before this, where I was. I've clearly just gotten here, but where did I arrive from?

Anoinda's hands deftly remove my one article of clothing, and then they traverse down my waist. "Ooh, it is good to see you again!" she says to my cock. It doesn't even seem to notice her. My mind is somewhere else.

With *someone* else.

But who? I groan and rub the side of my head, snatching the loincloth back.

"I'm not in the mood," I hiss, and walk to a corner far from the fountain in the center of the mezzanine. Anoinda huffs with annoyance and trots back to whatever rat king of fucking she was a part of before.

I have this aching feeling like whatever it is I can't remember is very important, and it's just out of my reach.

Someone. I know it was a someone. A master of mine, perhaps. What was I doing before I found myself in the hall of the gods? I haven't come here in a long time. As the other gods have been forgotten and disappeared, so has the hall gone quiet. But now it is bursting with noise and activity again.

But there is one god absent. My mother.

I stand up suddenly and look around the room. She's not among those collected here, but my father is. He's watching me with interest, his black hair spread out long and thick behind him.

Lucia is the only reason I can think of for why I'm here. She is the one who always called us together, and she is the only one not present, which must mean my foggy head is her doing.

After a time, my father gets to his feet and approaches me, carrying a decanter full of wine. The red liquid sloshes as he sits next to me.

My mother might have carved me from stone and given me life, but the god of the sea, Terano, is the one who created the stone that would eventually become me. A cup appears in my hands, and Terano pours wine into it. Where Lucia is impulsive and often petty, he is steadfast and quiet. But his rages, oh, they can be immense.

"This place is not what you think it is," he says. Then he urges me to take a drink of the wine. For some reason, I'm repulsed by it. This is the nectar of the gods, but what I find myself wanting is peasant's wine, rough and tart.

"I'm not supposed to be here," I say, and no words have ever felt truer. This is wrong. Being among these flawless, beautiful immortals, I feel like a stranger. I'm longing for something that isn't here.

Terano places a firm hand on my shoulder. "It's a difficult thing to accept," he says. "That they have forgotten you."

I turn to him. Surely that's not what's happened.

"No," I say firmly. "I know that's not true. If mortals are anything, it is greedy and incapable, and someone will always need a servant in me."

My father shakes his head. "This is not the real hall of the gods," he says, gesturing around us. "But we're meant to think that it is. Most of us just pretend that's where we are, because it makes it easier for the mind than knowing we have been sent to oblivion."

Forgotten. I can't be. Not when someone is out there, someone just on the edge of my memory who makes my heart race and my cock twitch. I don't know who it is, but they're not here—which means I shouldn't be, either.

"I have to go back." I toss down the wine and it spills across the shining white floor, the golden goblet bouncing off the floor with a loud *clang*. A few other gods look up to gawk at my outburst. "I need to get back to wherever I just came from!"

Terano sighs, and it's ripe with pity.

"That's not possible, Kireth. You don't leave this place. None of us do."

But I have to. He doesn't understand.

"Of course I can leave," I say tartly. I kick the cup aside and head for the doors. I pull on the handles... and they don't open.

A hush has fallen on the room as everyone watches me try the doors again. I yank and pull, harder and harder, until I'm grunting and gasping with effort.

My father's hand lands on mine.

"It's impossible," he says, his voice sad. "This is the end, Kireth. I'm sorry."

Chapter Fourteen

FAELA

When I wake up again, my body feels light—impossibly so, as if there's no weight attached to me at all.

The sky overhead is blue, a pure, bright, robin's-egg blue, untouched by even a wisp of cloud. There's a fresh smell in the air, as if it has only just rained, but that's impossible.

I sit up, which takes no effort at all despite the pain I was in only moments ago. Tall golden grass surrounds me, but it's perfectly soft, like a cloud. I get to my feet and find that my dress, while still looking like my dress, is clean and shining as if it were brand new. My hands are clean, too, with not a speck of dirt under the nails.

Is this what it's like to be dead?

I turn around in a circle, searching for any sign of Lucia. But I don't see the goddess anywhere.

Lifting my skirt so it doesn't tangle in the grass, I start walking. There must be something out here, some direction

I'm supposed to go in order to find Kireth. Not that there are any signposts.

Picking a direction, I walk and walk, not even feeling the grass against my legs. It's as if my body isn't actually here—there's no warm sun on my face even though it's bright daylight out. There's no gentle brush of breeze on my shoulders. It all just feels like... nothing.

The longer I walk, the less certain I become that I'm not simply dreaming. Perhaps Lucia sent me to the wrong place. The infinite landscape stretches on in every direction without a tree or mountain to be seen. I consider turning around to walk the other way, but now I'm not sure which direction I came from.

So instead, I keep walking, hoping that I'm not trapped here forever in this nothing land.

Perhaps it's only been a few minutes, or perhaps a few hours—I can't be sure, because the sun doesn't move—but soon the land starts changing. Some trees appear, and the grass turns greener. It almost feels... familiar. I can make out the shadow of mountains off in the distance, so I pick up my pace and keep going. Perhaps I need to get there, to that range up ahead.

As I move faster, a house appears, and then an orchard. Now I definitely recognize it. This is my neighbor's orchard, down the long road that leads into town. I sprint past the trees toward the house, looking for the older couple who live there.

But there's no one around. The house is empty.

Perplexed, I find the road and continue toward my farm. How did I end up back here, in my village? Aren't I dead? If so, what a peculiar afterlife.

There are cows and sheep in the pasture, and they look strong and healthy. But I don't recognize them—none of the patterns on the cows are right. Somehow there are cows here, but they aren't my cows.

The same is true for the crops. Green sprouts everywhere, but the stalks aren't planted in the same order as they are on my own farm. The house, too, looks different—clean and straight, as if it was just built. There are no collapsing stairs or shutters falling off the windows. It's as if it's been reborn, just like my dress.

As I approach, the front door opens. I haven't seen anyone around since arriving in the village, so it takes me by surprise when a woman steps out of the house.

My breath stops in my throat.

"Mother?"

It can't really be her. But there she is, standing in the doorway, waving both arms at me with a big smile on her face.

"Faela!" She comes down the stairs and embraces me in the middle of the pathway. "Oh, darling! I'm so glad you're back safely."

"Back?" I ask. "Back from where?"

"You went to the village to get some fresh bread. Where is the bread, by the way?" She eyes my empty hands, then grins in a carefree way I only remember from when I was small. "Did you see someone handsome and get distracted?"

I stare at her for a long time, not sure what to say. How much have I wished I could see her again, alive and hale, and here she is. But none of this makes sense. Is this my real mother, waiting for me in the afterlife?

She stands there waiting for an answer.

"Sorry." I give her an apologetic smile. "I did get distracted."

Mother pats me on the shoulder and leads me into the

house. "No problem. I have dinner cooking. Are you hungry?"

Oh, how I've missed her cooking. I'm quite a slouch in comparison.

"Starving," I say on reflex, and she guides me to a chair at the table. All the chairs are here, not a single one smashed to kindling against a wall. Mother returns to the pot she has boiling over the fire and stirs it, then ladles out a spoonful and sniffs.

"It'll be a good stew," she says, but I can't smell anything. I'm just so glad to see her, busying about, that I think little of it. She looks simply radiant, full of life, and for a moment I feel like I could just forget everything that's happened the last few years. I could just be here, with Mother, with our strange cows that aren't quite our cows, our crops that aren't quite our crops, in this house that isn't falling apart.

Soon the food is done, and Mother has been chatting the whole time about some neighborly gossip. She puts a bowl in front of me, and it makes my mouth water.

"Remember to let it cool down first," she says with an affectionate chuckle. "I know how you like to burn your tongue."

So I patiently wait while the stew cools, and then spoon some into my mouth.

I taste nothing. I chew and swallow, confused at how Mother's special soup could have no flavor to it.

"Good?" she asks, her hands clasped.

I force a grateful smile. "Yes. It's great."

Once we're finished eating the nothing-food, Mother pulls out her sewing. She shows off the new dress she's making for me so I don't have to wear the same one every day. It's made of a fine yellow fabric, certainly too fine for us. I simply watch as she talks and sews, telling me about which cows gave the most milk today, and which crops should come in first. I listen attentively, soaking up the familiar sound of her voice. It's as if she's been alive here all this time.

Still, as I clean up the dinner dishes, the sun outside remains high in the sky. Shouldn't it be setting soon? I stare through the kitchen window, an eerie tickle under my skin.

When I finish, Mother gets up and stretches. "It's time for bed," she says, and heads toward the stairs. "Won't you go to bed, Faela?"

I nod, though I'm not tired in the least. Going to bed in this house, knowing my mother is safe and sound? How many days have I dreamed of such a thing?

"Of course," I say.

We both change into our nightclothes, and once I'm under my blankets, Mother comes in to kiss me on the cheek. I let her do it without complaint.

"I'm glad you're back," she says, a familiar softness in her eyes. "I love you."

"I love you too, Mother."

She gives me one last kiss before leaving for her own room.

I close my eyes and try to sleep, even though bright sunlight is streaming in through the window.

I know this is wrong. All of it is wrong. But being here with my mother again... I see a beautiful glimmer of the life we could have had if the curse had never come. It is as wonderful as it is strange, beautiful while making me wonder what price I am paying.

Surely I came here for a reason. But what reason was that?

Soon, despite the light outside, sleep takes me.

THE SUN IS STILL at its zenith when I wake up the next morning. Mother is already outside working with the animals. When I join her, the temperature is perfect—still and calm as a warm spring day. My mother gives me a full, wide, wonderful smile when I appear, and hands me the chicken feed. I had forgotten how it looked to see my mother smile in only a few short years.

Had I really started to forget her? What an awful daughter I am, to let that smile fade from my memory. The sound of her voice brings everything rushing back, and I remember the way she turned chores into a game when I was young and once scared off a wolf by yelling and waving her arms. I remember how a boy made me cry, and Mother hugged me and made me a blackberry pie to help me feel better. Though my heart was still tender, so were the blackberries, and by the time night fell I'd forgotten all about him.

When Mother hugs me now, though, I can't really feel the weight of her arms. It's like only my mind is here, and everything else is my imagination running wild. But I'm so pleased to simply be with her again, hearing her voice and seeing her face, that I brush it aside.

By the end of the day, I'm struggling to remember how I got here. Why did I die in the first place? Am I really dead? Perhaps the last few years were simply an awful dream, and this is reality as it should have been.

But there's a tickle in the back of my mind that I'm missing something.

"Mother," I ask after dinner. "Once you told me a story about the lord in the forest, who will do one hundred tasks for those who ask."

She glances over while she makes a pastry. Perhaps it will be blackberry pie.

"Yes, of course!" She winks. "I have heard he's quite beautiful. Skin like stone, bearing the horns of a ram and those of a goat, with the face of a god. But he is also a trickster. The tales all say he will try however he can to misunderstand your requests."

"What was his name?" I ask. This is important. I know it is.

She rubs her chin. "I believe it was... Kireth."

Yes, of course. *Kireth*. Surely I couldn't forget.

"What of him?" Mother asks.

"Once you taught me the words to summon him."

She cocks her head. "Yes. But that is a legend, honey."

I know they were in a little book we kept. I go to the bookshelf and search for it, but I don't recognize any of the books. Their spines are blank, and when I pull them out, so are the covers. Inside, the pages are new and unmarked.

"This is wrong," I murmur to myself, replacing the book on the shelf. This house... it is not *my* house.

"What is it, honey?" Mother calls out. She's patting the dough into a ball and fetching her rolling pin.

"Nothing," I say, and return to the table. That bright, bright sunlight is still outside, never relenting. I feel unsettled after the blank books.

"Mother? Do you know where we are?"

Pausing, she turns to look at me. "What do you mean? We're at home, on the farm."

I point out the window. "How come the sun never sets?"

This time, she frowns. "Well, it's daytime now, honey."

Is she being obtuse on purpose? Or does she not know?

"But it was up last night when we went to bed," I say, trying to sound reasonable.

"Well, that's silly." She pulls out a dish and carefully carries the dough over to it, laying it across the bottom. "The sun doesn't shine at night."

"I know." I'm starting to feel impatient. "That's why it struck me as odd."

My mother fills the pie, but the berries are the wrong color. "Nothing seemed unusual to me."

"Mother," I finally ask. "Are you real? Are you dead, too?"

She spins around. "What? Honey, what sort of questions are these?" She sits down on the chair next to mine and puts one arm around my shoulders. "We are very well and alive, you and me. Look." She stares into my eyes, and I see my own hazel reflected back at me. "We're both here, together. That's all I've ever wanted. Aren't you happy?"

But something in her gaze feels off. Flat. This isn't my real mother.

No, I'm here for a different reason, I know it. Something is pulling me away from this house, from this strange woman who looks and sounds so familiar.

"Tell me the words again," I say to her, knowing this is important. "The words to summon Kireth."

She frowns at me. "Now why would I do that? We don't need him. We can handle the farm on our own."

But I know in my bones that I need him. My heart is certain that I shouldn't be here, that I was searching for something else. As much as I wish I could have my mother back, this house, this woman, those cows with different names—they are not mine.

"Kireth," I repeat, turning the word over in my mind. He's the key to the puzzle, I'm sure of it. I remember flashes of him running through grasses, bathing in the river, lying on top of me as he carefully made love to me.

How is that possible? Surely that can't be me with an ancient god. But I can feel that it's real—as if his weight is still pressing me down into the bed. But why is he not here? Why aren't we together now?

Then it hits me. I'm here for Kireth. I'm going to find him and take him back home with me, to our rickety house with the weak spot in the floor. We will play in the river and tend the farm together and enjoy each other's bodies in the grass.

Throwing away my love for him won't bring my mother back.

I stand up from the chair and push it in. Mother follows me with an inquisitive, slightly worried expression.

"I'm sorry," I say. "I know you're not my mother." This must be some trick of Lucia's to keep me from my true goal.

Mother chuckles uneasily. "What do you mean, sweet pea? Of course I'm your mother."

"You're not." As much as I wish she were. "Perhaps you don't even know it. I'm not sure what you are, exactly, but I'm not here to live out a fantasy that can't exist." It feels like a weight is sliding off my shoulders. "You're dead, Mother."

And isn't it time that I let her go?

She opens her mouth as if to speak, but nothing comes out. Then she reaches toward me with one hand, seeking me out, asking one last time if I'll take it.

I turn around and walk out the front door because I can't watch any longer. Wherever I need to go to find Kireth, I'd better start looking now.

Chapter Fifteen

KIRETH

I can't tell if time is passing fast or slow. Every hour feels exactly the same as the one before it. The other gods drink wine, eat fresh fruit and perfectly cooked lamb, and fuck often. I sleep more than not, hoping that if I can just pass the time, the memories will return to me.

All I know is that my heart is longing for something, craving something, and it isn't here. Whatever it is, whoever it is—that is where my purpose lies, and this place is standing in the way.

"What troubles you so much?" Terano asks, leaning against the edge of the fountain as he drops a strawberry into his open mouth. The strawberry is not red, but purple, and the sight of it unsettles me. No one else seems to think these things are odd, and I feel more alone now than I ever did for the hundreds of years I spent entombed in my temple.

"I'm not supposed to be here," I say, for what feels like the tenth time. "This isn't right." I can't explain how I know it, but I do. Whatever happened, I'm positive that my mother had something to do with it.

"That feeling will fade," my father assures me. "Get comfortable, Kireth. It is foolish to desire what you cannot have."

I don't answer, because there's nothing I can say to dissuade him. He is the unyielding ocean, after all.

"There is someone coming up the mountain!" Anoinda stands high up on one of the platforms, completely naked, as she peers out one of the great windows. "Look! Down there."

The other immortals are too sluggish with food and wine and pleasure to make it there in any quick fashion, but I hop to my feet and run up the steps to take a peek for myself.

Far below, the mountain levels out into a great, endless field. A small figure steadily climbs the rocky slope, one heavy step at a time. As the figure gets closer, I can just make out a long brown dress. Whoever she is, she hikes with one side of the dress held up in her hand, so it doesn't catch.

Something about that gesture, the way this strange interloper carries the hem as she clambers over the next rock, is eerily familiar.

"It's a mortal," Anoinda whispers, awed. "What would a mortal be doing here?"

Terano crosses his arms. "Perhaps she is lost. Though I don't know how a mortal would have come this far, not without help."

Help. Yes, she would have needed help. And there's only one goddess I know who isn't present here, who would have the power to bring a mortal to this realm.

What is Lucia meddling in?

The mortal woman slips on a rock and stumbles, and I catch myself reaching toward her. Whoever she is, I don't want anything bad to happen to her.

"What is she coming here for?" one of the others asks over my shoulder. He reeks of wine. "This is the hall of gods. She has no place here."

But I don't think she is coming to drink our wine or eat our strange food.

Eventually, she disappears underneath the great hall, and we are all left to wonder if she has reached the peak or not. I watch for a soft body falling from the rocks, but there is silence.

When the other immortals grow bored, they disperse and return to their debauched activities. But I don't leave the platform, watching and waiting, wondering why this strange creature is here.

I don't know how much time passes before there comes a small knock at the heavy doors of the hall. Terano stands up, a mystified look on his face. If they do not open, how could someone be let inside?

He heads toward the doors, but I'm there before he is. This time, when I pull the handles, they open with a heavy creak.

Standing in the doorway is a young woman with bright hazel eyes, her brown hair wafting behind her. When she sees me, she smiles.

"Kireth." The way she says my name, a sense of recognition flutters through me. The cobwebs in my mind are blowing in the wind, clinging to the walls.

"Who are you?" I ask. Her dress is so plain, she looks as if she came here from a peasant's hovel.

The happiness in her eyes at seeing me fades. "Don't you remember me, Kireth? I'm Faela. I came to get you."

"But I don't know you," I say, though I feel like perhaps I used to.

She shakes her head, disbelieving. "But you do know me." She reaches toward me, and instinctively, I back away.

What is a mortal doing in this realm? Was she sent here to test me?

It's as if I can see her heart breaking on her face. Whoever she is, she certainly knows me. I wonder if I had an affair with her hundreds of years ago and it's simply slipped my mind.

"Why don't you let our guest in?" Terano suggests gently, opening the door wider. "Please, enter, mortal. You have had a long journey."

I step to the side as the woman bows her head deeply. "Thank you," she says, then steps over the threshold. She looks up at my father, her eyes wide. "Forgive me, but who are you?"

His laugh comes out a bellow. "Of course, she does not remember me. That is why I'm here, after all." He slaps his belly. "I am Terano, god of the sea. And you have reached the hall of the gods."

Her little mouth falls open, and a few of the other immortals have a laugh at her expense.

"Would you like some wine, dear Faela?" my father asks.

The woman glances at me, as if unsure what to do—and hoping I will help her.

"Do as you like," I say, waving a hand. Her brows crease, like she had hoped for a different answer.

"Then, please, join us." Terano closes the door behind her with a thud. "It has been some time since I enjoyed the company of a mortal."

The other gods surround her, all curious about this creature that's wandered into our midst. I don't like watching them fawn and gawk, but I have no say over what becomes of this human visitor. She keeps glancing over at me as naked gods come down from their nests to marvel at her, and I sense her distress.

It's when Lavis, the god of misdeeds, pulls up the hem of her dress and causes her to shriek that I intervene.

"Leave her be," I growl, plucking his hands away. I won't let her be touched like this. The other gods back away, and Terano chuckles.

"Perhaps this mortal is spoken for," he says mischievously.

Anoinda flashes me an irritated look. "Is this why you won't play with me, Kireth?" she asks, grabbing the mortal's arm. "You've got a hard-on for this plain human girl?"

A fire I didn't know existed is stoked inside me. I shove Anoinda, hard, and the other gods gasp as she stumbles back. I take the stranger's hand and lead her away from the cluster of nosy fools, toward a set of stairs on the far end of the hall. Reluctantly, she follows me.

"Kireth?" she asks, tentative. "Where are you taking me?"

"Away from these bumbling idiots."

It wasn't too many centuries ago that I was one of them, but now they seem like idle, stupid courtesans. The woman doesn't ask anything else as I guide her up the steps, toward one of the platforms with a curtained room. Inside, a goddess is moaning while another has her face buried between her legs.

"Kireth?" the first immortal says. "Are you joining us?"

"Get out." I rip open the curtain and point. They both glare at me. "Get out! Now!"

There are huffs of annoyance as they pull themselves apart and hurry off the bed.

"Asshole," one of them mumbles while they gather their clothes and storm out through the curtain.

Then it's just me and the mortal standing on either side of the mussed bed. She nervously rubs her hands together, glancing at the bed and then at me.

"Why are you here?" I ask, pulling the curtains closed. The room descends into a warm, dim darkness, a floating flame up by the ceiling the only light.

When she turns to me, her face strikes me as painfully familiar. In her own strange, plain way, she is beautiful—almost otherworldly.

"I'm here for you." She slides both her legs onto the bed and folds them underneath her, and I am almost certain that I've seen this same girl do this same thing before.

"How do I know you?" It's not a matter of whether or not I know her—I'm sure now that our paths have crossed before. But what could have possibly brought her here, to oblivion, looking for me?

She fiddles with the hem of her dress. "I summoned you once."

Ah, so she was one of my masters. Perhaps I did more than one kind of task for her, if you know what I mean, and that's why I find myself so eager to protect her.

She slides toward me on the bed, taking my hand in hers, and this time I don't pull away.

"Have you really forgotten how you saved me?" she asks, her big eyes wide.

"Saved you?" I echo. That's silly. I don't go around saving foolish humans.

She twines her fingers with mine. "It's true. You found what was wrong with my farm. You cured it." There's a shyness in her eyes now. "And you taught me so many things."

As the timbre of her voice drops, my blood abruptly rushes southward. I hold in a gasp when my cock twitches under my loincloth, triggered by the mere sound. Her hand trails up my arm, just tiny, gentle ghost touches that seem timid on the surface but belie a deeper passion. When I remain still, she continues that gentle movement upward until she reaches my shoulder, then my chest. Her hand finally stops over my heart.

"What sort of things did you learn from me?" I ask, my voice catching. Was she a lonely widow who came to me for companionship?

"Well, the first thing you taught me was how to be specific." A smile teases her lips. "How to give clear instructions."

"That sounds like me."

Her hand drifts down to the swirling designs on my skin, and my flesh trembles underneath her fingers.

"You never did teach me the words, though," she says, a touch of sadness in her tone.

I'm surprised. Few have ever tried to dismiss me. Usually, they flail and threaten and roar with their displeasure until they learn how to be smarter with their requests.

"Did you want to learn them?" I ask. "I can tell you now. Not that it will do you much good. Since I'm here, I cannot return to my temple again. My time on the mortal plane is up."

Her hand stops moving, then tightens into a fist. When she lowers her head, I can see tears dotting her cheeks like gemstones.

This baffles me more than anything.

"Why are you crying, mortal?" I ask her. I want to reach

out and wipe them away, and my belly twists at the thought of being the one to make her cry.

When she gazes up at me and brings her hand to my cheek, I stay still. Her palm is warm and so, so gentle, the way a newborn calf might lip at you hoping for food. Her finger traces my cheekbone down to my lips. The motion makes my cock twitch again, and I realize just how hard I've gotten under my loincloth.

For this small slip of a human woman? And yet she is tantalizing, with soft skin that looks infinitely kissable, and a pink mouth that seems like it would welcome me inside if I got the chance. Reflexively I lick my lips, wondering what she would taste like.

"I'm crying," she says, "because I'm imagining how good kissing you would feel."

"Oh?" I preen a little at this. "You enjoy the idea? Well, you should try, then."

The playful god in me rises up, curious about this woman who seems to desire me. I have been desired by many mortals, but from this quiet, shy one, it would feel like a gift.

She sits up fully and tugs me toward her. Perhaps I misjudged and there is more to this girl than meets the eye.

I swoop down and take her lips in mine quickly, so she can't change her mind. I mean it to be a small peck, a light tease just to humor her—but the faint taste of her strikes a chord deep inside me. Her mouth responds immediately, taking my lower lip in hers, sucking on it gently, running her tongue across it like she has practiced this many times. How does she know just the way I like to kiss? My tail weaves around my side, drawn to her, entranced by her. It brushes down her hip, curling under the curve of her ass. She gasps and leans into it as she kisses me again, more forcefully this time, and her hands wind around my neck to draw me closer.

How does one woman taste so good? She's like a summer honeysuckle, delicate and sweet, and I lower her to the bed so I can get a bigger gulp of her. She falls with me, her body easily molding to mine, giving underneath me in all the right places. Her hands roam up through my hair to my horns, as if she knows them, is familiar with them. I sense that her hands recognize me better than I recognize myself.

"Kireth," she murmurs into my neck, and then she places a small butterfly kiss there. "I know what I want. I know what I need now."

"And what is that, sweet girl?" I ask her, and the words glide off my tongue as if I've said them a hundred times before.

She smiles, peering at me from under long lashes. "You."

Chapter Sixteen

KIRETH

My whole body shivers. Somehow I know these are the words I want to hear, even if I don't understand why. This plain peasant wants me, only me, and I find that I want her, too. I want to keep tasting her heady flavor, keep drinking in her lovely smell, keep exploring her effervescent body. If what she desires is me, then I will grant her wish, and perhaps it will grant mine, too.

I move my kisses from her plush mouth to her jaw, and when she tilts her head back, I drop to her long throat. Her back arches, pressing her breasts into my chest. My arms slide under her, keeping her anchored to me as I kiss her collarbone. I could simply eat her, bring her inside me, know her as I know myself. The enormity of this desire overwhelms me, and my hips slide across hers, my cock dragging against her thighs. She inhales sharply, and the mound of her pelvis rises off the bed to grind against me. I'm almost delirious with gratification that she lusts for me, too. This quiet creature is sensual and thirsty, as tantalizing as she is demure, and I sense these are only two sides of her many multitudes.

I would like to know more of them. Perhaps all of them.

My hands slide down over her pert rear, cupping it tight, making sure my length is nudging between her legs. Instinctively she spreads them for me, and now I need nothing more than to remove the starchy brown dress keeping us apart.

I draw back from her, and my mortal whimpers at our separation.

"Don't worry," I murmur in her ear as I grab the hem of her dress. I draw it up over her strong, creamy thighs, and she eagerly shifts on the bed to let me slip it up her body and over her head. Of course, there is more underneath—humans love to wrap up their bodies in so many pointless layers. But her hazel eyes never stray from mine as she peels off the last of her clothing herself, revealing her to me.

The soft globes of her breasts hang low on her chest, her nipples perfect pinnacles, taut with her arousal. My hands find their way toward them without my conscious command, as if they long to take those perfect breasts in my palms and lessen the burden. The woman's eyes are hooded as my thumbs brush over just the tips of her nipples, and a wisp of a breath escapes her lips.

"Kireth." My name on her tongue makes my hair stand up on end. "Please."

I don't need anything else. I seize her breast in my mouth, just over her rapidly beating heart, and smooth my hand across her belly toward the crux of her thighs. They open in anticipation. As my hand slips between them, she lets out a breathy moan. I drag my teeth over her nipple, one and then the other, before I dip into her soft heat.

I'm shocked by how wet I find her, how readily her body is already weeping for me, as if it knows what I plan to do. As I run the pad of my finger over her sensitive clit, her hips buck, and she moans lavishly underneath me. I swipe over it again and again as I suckle her breasts, relishing how her body reacts to every taste.

But the more I tease her, the more I find that I'm teasing myself, and I don't know how much more I can stand. She hasn't even touched me and yet my cock is drooling for her, wetting the fabric of my loincloth, as if my body already knows what it will find inside her and it wants for nothing else.

At last, I dip a finger into her opening, and she wriggles underneath me, eager and accepting. How smoothly I'll fit inside her, I think, twitching at the mere suggestion. She is so small, so tight, that the squeeze of her around me could very well be my undoing.

I want to be undone by this strange mortal.

Her little hands reach down to untie my loincloth, and then my cock is free, sloping toward her in a way that I'm certain will fit perfectly inside her. I thrust my finger into her wet heat, testing her, opening her up for me, and her delicious gasps turn into thick moans.

It's time to feel her for myself. Her hands wrap around my shaft, but I shake my head.

"No," I tell her, withdrawing so I can move down her body to the wide gap of her thighs. "This is how you should feel me."

She stares down at where I'm dripping my anticipation onto her soft cunt, then rapidly nods.

"Yes," she agrees. "That's how."

I want to take her slowly. I want to test the waters, work her like an adventurer on a great quest. But as I pull her lower lips apart with the head of my cock, just circling her center, I'm not sure if I can.

"Do it," she urges me. "Bring me there, Kireth. I want to go with you."

Her body gives easily as I guide myself inside her, and she's warm and slippery for me.

Oh. The sensation of her is heavenly. I've never felt anything so pure and full of life as her cunt. I could drown in it, in her, and happily never come back up for air. I kiss her furiously as I fall into her depths.

"My sweet farm girl," I say, the words tumbling out of me of their own accord. Why am I saying them as if I know her, this woman who came knocking at the door of the gods?

Because I do. When her gaze meets mine, her mouth open in a moan of pleasure, I remember her.

My Faela. She's found me.

I can only hope that she's forgiven me, too.

FAELA

My god. My immortal. My Kireth.

There are no words to describe how it feels to be joined with him again, to have his perfect, lithe body on top of mine. He's limitless, thrusting so deep inside me that I can't imagine there's anywhere left for him to go.

He's staring into my eyes now as he drives ever further, and I'm certain that at last, he recognizes me. I don't know what spell Lucia cast to place this obstacle in my way, but we have surpassed it together.

Kireth's motions become feverish and irregular as he encircles me with his arms, bringing my face into the curve of his neck. There, he clutches me tight as he gives me all of himself, and through his groans, I can hear my name muttered over and over. I know it's him, really him, because he's tipping his hips and aiming for the place he knows I love, that one red-hot spot where each stroke of that marvelous cock triggers a bone-deep blast of pleasure. I'm crying out for him, my legs flung tight around his waist, drawing him farther and farther inside me as that tension in my belly grows. Feverishly he pumps, his sweat dripping down onto my forehead as he groans and pries me ever wider. There was a void inside me that's now filled, and I never want to imagine my world without him.

"Yes," he murmurs into my ear as I writhe and moan, trying desperately to release. "Come for me, my beautiful woman."

He slams into me hard and his cock grows even fuller, swelling with his own end. Every string in me is stretched to its limit, and suddenly, they all snap.

My thighs clench as I suck him inside so that we never have to be apart again. Kireth heaves with the force of his climax and it drags me along with it, into that bottomless place that's reserved just for us.

There is no bounty so great as being loved by a god.

Spent, Kireth wraps his arms around my middle and rolls us over, our legs tangled, his dripping cock still wedged firmly where it belongs. He nuzzles my hair, feeling all along the edges of my body with his hands as if he can't believe that I'm real.

"You came for me," he whispers. "My Faela."

"I had to." I brush the curve of his horn with one hand, just remembering him, memorizing him. "When she took you away..." I ache just thinking of it, how the last words I'd spoken to him were so hateful. "I need you. I love you. I don't want to do all of this—existing—without you."

He fervently kisses the top of my head, and I can feel his heart hammering in his chest. "I would never leave you. But I'm not sure that you can stay here, either." There's defeat in his voice.

"Then come with me." I hold him even closer. "Return to the farm with me."

"I don't think I can." He shakes his head, letting out a heavy, unsteady breath. "This place... I can't leave it. I am trapped here. I cannot go back with you."

Dread settles over me. Did Lucia really send me all this way, taunt me with the possibility of saving him, only to find he's locked inside a prison?

"That can't be right." I bury my face in his neck. "That's not what she told me."

"Who told you?" Kireth's voice fills with suspicion. "Was it my mother?"

Before I can answer, there's a crash, and a few shouts rise up. We unspool our bodies from each other, and Kireth pushes aside the curtain to look.

He freezes, his mouth hanging slack. "Lucia?"

I grab my slip and put it on over my head as Kireth gapes. Far down below us, the doors have been opened wide. With a carefree confidence, Lucia strolls in.

"Ah, Kireth." Her eyes crinkle at the edges as she smiles up at us. "And the farm girl. You made it."

The doors fall closed behind her.

Once my dress is on, we walk hand in hand down the steps to the mezzanine, where the great fountain in the center happily burbles. There's a knowing smirk on Lucia's face as we approach together, Kireth's hand inside mine. He might be a god, but Lucia frightens even him.

"You made it past my obstacle," she says to me with one eyebrow arched, her lip curled. "You're not as stupid as you look."

"Mother," Kireth warns.

She chortles. "And you, my wayward child, got caught in the web of a mortal. You found your chosen one, when none of these other high and mighty gods never could have dreamed of it."

The god who tried to pull up my dress before glares in my direction. "Kireth, of all of us?" he says, spitting on the floor.

"Despite my spell, you remembered her." Lucia shakes her head, wearing a rueful smile. "I've done my best, but you've defeated me."

Kireth squeezes my hand tighter. "Are you going to let us leave now?"

"But you are an immortal," she says, tilting her head at him like he's an odd bug she found on the ground. "Now that you're here, you cannot leave, just like Terano cannot leave, either." There's a wistfulness in her voice. "And now, neither can I."

"You've been forgotten, too," Kireth says. She just nods her head in my direction, as if she expected it. As if now that I'm dead, there's no one left to remember her name.

"Are you saying I can't take him back with me?" I demand. "After all this?"

Lucia shrugs. "You are mortal. You can open and close these doors as you like and cross over the threshold." She grins widely at Kireth. "But immortals? We are bound here for the rest of time."

Chapter Seventeen

KIRETH

I'm stuck here.

I can't return to the house with the sagging roof. I can't tend to the crops, or pet Petal's head, or taste my Faela's delicious cunt.

I can't go *home*.

Her hands cling tight to mine. "That can't be right," she says, taking a step closer to Lucia. "He has to be able to come with me. I came all this way for him. You sent me here! You told me I could get him back!"

She is fierce, my Faela. But all the life has drained out of me. There is no defying oblivion.

"I did, didn't I?" says Lucia thoughtfully. She rubs her chin, tilting her head. "Perhaps, if Kireth were mortal like you, he could step through the door."

Faela stomps her foot. "But he's not! We all know that. He's..." She turns to me. "He's a god."

Then it occurs to me what my mother is trying to say.

"If I were to give up immortality..." I bring Faela tight against my side. "Could I go then?"

Lucia's face transforms into a smile. "I knew I'd created you to have quicker wits than that," she says proudly. Then her tone grows more serious. "You could. You would be shackled to a mortal life, Kireth. You would grow old and die, as you never have."

Faela is speechless. I wonder what it would be like to get old. To age as mortals do, to watch my body change and deteriorate, to look death in the eyes and fall into it.

"Kireth," Faela whispers. "You can't." Her hand clenches mine tight.

I squeeze hers back. "But I can."

Yes, I can stay with my farm girl for as long as our short lives will allow. I can love her until she's old and gray and we have a different dog with a different name.

"And I will give it up," I say with a certainty. "I will throw my immortality away, if it means we can go home."

My mother gives me a sad smile. "I thought that might be what you chose."

"But you would lose everything!" Faela's eyes are red with unshed tears. "You would die someday. You would become—"

"Like you?" I push some of her rogue brown hair behind her ear. "I can imagine no better thing."

Tilting her chin up, I lean down and brush my lips over hers in a brief, gentle promise of what might come later. Her pulse speeds up under my hand at just this small touch. How wonderful it will be to spend a lifetime teasing her this way.

Behind us, Terano shakes his head. "Lucia," he chides. "Always playing your games, even with your children."

"Hmph." She waves him off. "It worked, didn't it? Now Kireth." She puts one hand on each of my shoulders. "After this, you will walk through these doors and never return. When you die, you will go to the place all mortals do. We won't see you again."

I think that perhaps there are even some unshed tears in her eyes.

With a nod, I say, "I understand."

Lucia tilts her head back and begins to hum. The air vibrates around us. I feel a sudden slackening in my muscles, as if the energy is being drained out of them. Faela gasps and rushes to my side as I fall over, boneless. It's as if my spirit is being drawn out through my mouth.

"Kireth!" Faela cries out.

My mother holds up her hand, and in it, there is a small, swirling ball of light. She blows on it, as if sending off a dandelion seed, and the light winks out.

Already, I can feel the creep of death on me—but it doesn't frighten me the way I thought it would. When I look down, my skin is no longer the gray of stone, but a light brown, full of flesh and blood.

"Are you all right?" Faela asks, helping me back to my feet.

"I'm fine now." I smile fully at her, at the girl I've chosen and who was chosen for me. "Let's go home."

I give my mother a kiss on the hand, and my father slaps my shoulder.

"I'm glad I got to see you before the end," Terano says. "Now go. Live your mortal life."

"Oh, I will." I anticipate with glee all the things I can do with it.

When I pull on the door handles, they open wide for

us. Taking Faela's hand in mine, I tug her over the threshold.

The moment we step through, the doors fall shut behind us with a resounding *clang!* Then, all of oblivion disappears behind us.

We are free.

FAELA

My immortal has chosen a life with an expiration date—for me. I don't think there's ever been such a declaration of love as that.

He has changed, too. His skin is a bright bronze, his hair as dark as before, but the ends are now tipped with sunlight. His horns and tail remain.

It's a long way back the way I came. I just hope that Lucia was right, and we'll return to the mortal plane where I came from.

At the bottom of the mountain, the farm and the village are gone. We walk through the endless yellow grasses, taking our time, relishing being together again. After much teasing and giggling, Kireth rolls me up in his arms and we fall to the ground together, our tongues dancing, our limbs exploring each other as if we've been separated for years. He pulls up my dress and pleasures me with his mouth, then slides his cock inside me like it was meant to fit there. I moan his name and he clutches me close, taking his time, prying one climax from my body after another.

We fall asleep like that, lying in the cloud-soft grasses, curled around each other.

When I wake up, it's because a wet tongue is swiping across my face.

"Petal?"

The dog's tail frantically wags as I sit up and wipe my cheek. Kireth's eyes open, and he rubs them with both fists.

We're lying in the sheep field, just down the hill from the house. The sky is darkening, and I'm relieved to see the sun moving across the sky after my short stay in the house that wasn't mine, with the mother that wasn't mine, either.

"We're home," I breathe. "Lucia brought me back like she promised."

"She might be a little naughty, but she never lies." Kireth stretches his arms like a cat, as if we've just woken from a most relaxing nap. His smile grows as he surveys the land around us. "Just like you left it."

It looks like less than a day on the farm has passed since I "died" and came back to life. Quickly, we feed the animals, who are restless after being cooped up, and attend to the crops. We're exhausted from playing catch-up by the time night falls, and Kireth grumbles at how much faster he gets tired.

Under the starry sky that night, Kireth and I sit together on the front steps of our home.

"Is it strange?" I ask. "Knowing there are no more gods?"

He shrugs as he sips some wine. "Our time was past. The world is changing. Soon, it will touch even this place, you know—we won't be able to avoid all those newfangled inventions they have down in the valley. It might even make our lives easier."

I don't like this thought. I want a simple life here,

rebuilding the farm and the house and the barn, lying in the grass under the perfect darkness of night.

"I can't believe an ancient god is telling me to modernize," I grumble.

He kisses my cheek and offers me some more wine. "Who knows? Maybe it will make us even happier."

THE NEXT MORNING, Kireth brings his hands to the base of a plant and starts to imbue it with his magic, intent on hurrying the harvest.

But nothing happens. His eyebrows crease, and he concentrates even harder.

"Why isn't it working?" He sits down in the dirt, tail slapping the ground with frustration.

I kneel next to him. "Your magic must have been tied to your immortality." I put an arm around his shoulders and run my hand through his wild hair, to the base of his horn. "But we don't need it anymore. *You* don't need it anymore."

Kireth sighs a deep, weary sigh, and leans into me. "I suppose I'll have to just rely on the water and the sun and the soil to do the work."

"Just like mortals have since the beginning of time," I say with a chuckle.

He shudders. "Mortal. I'm going to have to get used to that."

When we're finished with our work, we eat fresh berries and bread, cheese and wine to celebrate returning from the land of the dead with our hides intact. Soon my head is warm and fuzzy, and Kireth swings me up into his arms to carry me up the stairs.

He sways, nearly toppling over.

"Oops. You're a lot heavier when I don't have magic to help me."

I giggle. "Welcome to being human."

WE FALL into a pattern of life again: I see to the livestock, and Kireth tends to the crops. Every evening, we cook together and eat together, and Kireth likes to feed me blackberries and strawberries right from the basket. We repair the house and the fences, and with an extra pair of hands, we're able to expand the fields in use for farming, too.

I am wary of the curse that still lives in a wooden box in our home, so we go on a journey to the forest down below the mountain. Here, Kireth says goodbye to his temple for good, where he will never return.

Then we bury the box deep in the dirt, hoping it will remain there, undiscovered, for the rest of time.

KIRETH

I never could have imagined a life like this for myself. Even without my magic, it's a bliss that's almost beyond my understanding.

My sweet farm girl, with her twinkling hazel eyes and soft waves of brown hair, occupies every last corner of my heart. How I love watching her with a newborn lamb in her lap, or training one of the new dogs to round up cattle. In the winter, we plant crops to rejuvenate the soil, and spend many long, cold days inside finding new and inventive ways to warm ourselves up.

As the seasons pass, so do we both get older. It's a strange and foreign thing to feel my body get tired earlier, to watch the wrinkles appear on my Faela's face, to see them on my own in the mirror.

But I don't regret a single minute of it. I hope that when we die, we get to do it side by side, just as we lived.

Epilogue

S

FAELA

One of my favorite things is making my demon husband work a little for what he wants.

We finished our chores early today, and he wanted to fuck me in the barn on the hay. But I have bigger, better plans than that. When he swipes at the hem of my skirt, I duck out of the way and hurry out the barn doors, leaving him behind.

"Hey!" Kireth calls after me, glaring at my back. "Where are you going?" His cock is already thick and drooling and pulling hard at his loincloth.

"Good luck running with that!" I call back, and take off down the hill toward the river. I hear his gasp of annoyance behind me, and then the pounding of his feet as he gives chase. Races are much fairer now that he's mortal and doesn't have magic to rely on, but he still has longer legs and moves fast. I'll have to stay on my toes.

I race along the river until I reach the rocks, where I hop from one to the next to cross, then dart off into the woods. Kireth hollers from somewhere behind me.

"When I find you, I'm going to gobble you right up!"

I giggle and duck into some brush, the branches scraping at my legs and pulling on the fabric of my dress. Oops. Guess I'll have to do a little repair job later. I can hear his thundering footsteps now that he's no longer outfitted with the soft touch of a god, and it makes it easy to tell where he is and zigzag just out of his reach.

Unfortunately, I've gotten so wet between the legs just thinking about what he'll do when he catches me that my thighs are starting to chafe.

"Oooh, not such a sweet girl today, are you?" he calls out. "Maybe I can't find you with magic anymore, but I can still smell you!"

A shiver runs through me. He does love to bury his face in my pussy and snuffle it like a dog—he would know how I smell when I'm excited for him, when I'm thinking of his strong body and thick cock, and how good it feels when—

I'm startled out of my thoughts by a branch breaking, and Kireth leaps through the trees right in front of me. I screech and stumble backwards, but he catches me around the waist.

"There you are," he growls, pulling me closer to him, even as I wriggle in his arms. I've been caught. "I didn't think it was possible to want you even more, but if I don't put my cock inside you now, I think that mortal death might come for me sooner than I thought."

I want the same thing, of course, and now my blood is hot and pumping. I know exactly how to take him. I stumble to the nearest tree, hike up my dress to my hips, and lean against it.

"Oh, fuck," Kireth mutters to himself as he gazes down at my exposed rear. I expect him to slide his hungry cock inside me, but instead, I feel his hot breath against my pussy. On his knees in the dirt, he torments it with his tongue, and shoves two fingers inside my weeping slit. My head falls forward, and I moan as he pumps quickly, getting me even wetter. His other hand reaches up to my ass, and plying my cheeks apart, he starts to explore the puckered, much smaller hole there.

Is that what he's going to do today?

He wets his finger and adds it to the mix, so he's attacking me in both places at once while he wreaks havoc on my clit with his mouth, and it's not long before I'm gasping and squeezing and light bursts behind my eyes.

When I've recovered, I turn around to repay the favor, but Kireth wags a finger. "No. You got me too close by leading me on your little chase." He positions himself behind me. "I'm going to fill up your beautiful cunt so full you won't be able to hold any more."

My head falls forward as he brings his cock to my dripping entrance, and there he teases me with that soft head until I'm squirming and bucking my hips back against his. Then, ever so slowly, he slides in.

Oh, it will never cease to amaze me how good it feels when I'm full of him. Kireth starts slowly, never thrusting more than an inch or two, warming me up for him. Soon he plunges in deep, the head of his cock settling right where it belongs. I grip the tree as he hastens his pace, aiming for all the places that make my body sing, and I cry and scream as he pillages me faster and faster. Soon I'm stepping over the threshold and he's coming with me, our bodies melding into one as he slams inside me one last time.

"Sweet girl," he murmurs into my ear as he ejects all of

himself, his hot juices commingling with mine until they're leaking out onto the forest floor. I shudder and clench underneath him, my hands losing their grip on the tree as he pulls me against his chest. "I will never get enough of you."

We walk back to the river, hands linked, his seed dripping down my thighs. We abandon our clothes and get in the water together, where he tenderly washes my hair, my breasts, my hips, my thighs. Of course, he can't resist taking me one more time, and my cries fill the air.

When we're both finally spent, we lie on the riverbank naked and let our bodies dry.

"Faela," Kireth begins, voice tentative. He's almost always full of confidence, so it draws my attention.

"What is it?"

"Have you ever considered..." He trails off, clearly uncertain. "Did you ever want to have children?"

I must have a very startled look on my face, because Kireth quickly looks away. "Never mind."

"Wait." I roll onto my side and take his hand in mine. "Is that something you want?"

The thought has never crossed my mind, not since he first started brewing that potion for me. It's never come up, so I just assumed he wasn't interested.

Kireth shrugs, as if it's unimportant to him—but I can tell that it is.

"I don't know. I was just watching you with the new calves, and..." His tail is flicking in the air between us with excitement, even if his face doesn't show it. "I've never felt this before. Like I want to try it before we get too old."

I wonder what our baby might come out like.

"I've had children before," he says quickly, with some shame. "But I never got to know them. To see them. By the time I was summoned again, they had grown up and died." He runs a hand down my arm. "I want to be there. I want to see. If I go first, I don't want to leave you alone."

It's a dark thought, imagining one of us going before the other. Yet I don't want to leave him alone, either.

"All right." I scoot closer, trailing my fingers up his chest, then down again to his hips. "Let's do it."

His eyes widen. "Really?"

"Sure. It's a kind of immortality, in a way. They'll live on long after us and perhaps have children of their own. We'll never really be forgotten."

A wide smile crosses his playful face, and then it turns wicked. He jumps on top of me, pinning me down in the mud. "Perfect," he whispers, leaning down to nip my earlobe. "Can we start now?"

I sputter. "But I just drank the potion a few days ago—"

He cuts me off by kissing me. "Call it practice. Besides, I want to make a few of them."

"Lots of extra hands around the farm?" I ask, laughing as he trails his hands down to my nipples.

"Lots of bright little voices," he says, reaching down to guide his warm, leaking cock inside me once again, and I welcome him in.

Then I let him carry me away, off to a place I could only have imagined in my dreams.

Join My Newsletter!

For all the latest regarding books, and to get a FREE Trollkin Lovers novella, join my newsletter! You can also find signed paperbacks and artwork of your favorite books.

www.LyonneRiley.com

Get access to tons of NSFW artwork (including art of Faela and Kireth!) as well as my latest serial by subscribing on Patreon.

www.Patreon.com/LyonneRiley

About the Author

Lyonne Riley published her first book at age five, which was written on tiny sheets of notebook paper, and she insisted on giving a copy to everyone she knew. She's been writing ever since, from fan fiction in her teen years to original fiction as an adult. After a stint in traditional publishing, she discovered what she truly wanted to write: very smutty stories about monsters and the little humans they worship.

Now she lives in the middle of nowhere with her dogs and spouse, writing sexy fairy tales.

Acknowledgments

I would like to thank everyone involved in helping me through the process of putting out this book. I can't say enough how much I appreciate the help and encouragement of the people around me—especially Amber, who told me I could do this in the first place.

Huge thank you to Linda Noeran for the gorgeous cover illustration. To my critique partners, who gave me phenomenal feedback: You all make this possible. And of course, my amazing spouse, who has always supported my dreams—and given me lots of inspiration for my characters' sexy adventures.

I couldn't have done this without the expertise of my fellow self-published romance authors. Thank you for inviting me into your circles and helping me through this process.

And thank you to my readers, who gave this book a shot.